WalkTall
Izaic Yorks

ink & virtue

This is a work of fiction. Names, characters, places, and incidents either are the product of the author's imagination or are used fictitiously. Any resemblance to actual persons, living or dead, events, or locales is entirely coincidental.

Copyright © 2023 by Izaic Yorks

All rights reserved. No part of this book may be reproduced or used in any manner without written permission of the copyright owner except for the use of quotations in a book review. For more information, address: info@izaicyorks.com

First paperback edition November 2023

Book design by Izaic Yorks

ISBN 979-8-9873369-3-9 (paperback)

ISBN 979-89873369-4-6 (ebook)

www.izaicyorks.com

WHO IS THIS BOOK FOR?

Dear reader,

First and foremost, *Walktall* is set in the world of *Ascendant: Saga of Valor*. In one regard, it is meant to enrich that story and set easter eggs for fans who go on to read more in the series. If you have never read the aforementioned book you might wonder about established world-building—use of language, motifs, and references. I apologize to any new readers as I know that can be annoying. It is a purposeful choice made to honor established fans.

However, in another regard, it is meant for fresh eyes. This story is written in part to honor the real and ongoing struggle of people who are/have lived through the hell of a re-education camp. Within are real details of tactics and strategies used to break people down. These tactics work and are employed to this day. *Walktall* is not a light read in that way. Hours of research have yielded common themes that I hope to impart throughout the story. Namely, unexplained chaos and the suddenness with which these experiences end—in freedom or death. As you embark on this journey understand *why* and *resolution* are never of importance to survivors of these camps. Rather the story for them lies in the day-to-day. The moments of air before the stormy waters submerge them once again.

I hope you enjoy the read and if you have any feedback I always try my best to respond. I can be best reached at izaic@izaicyorks.com

Sincerely,

Izaic

DEDICATION

To my father, whom braved deep places for the sake of his family.

To my wife, the most loving and loyal companion I will ever meet this side of heaven.

WALKTALL

DEATH MEANS LOSING MY MIND - RESISTING MEANS FACING DEATH. SOMEHOW I SURVIVED.

Entering the abyss is easy. It's the leaving that's jarring

CONTENTS

A Strollers Story	XII
A Strollers Story Continued	XIII
Prologue	1
1. One Deep Night	6
2. Welcome to Vyesgors	15
Rule, First	18
3. Hair Harold	19
4. Light Gifts	26
5. Blood Money	34
6. I Believe In Magic	38
7. Common Language	44
8. Still Boys	50
9. Jealous Monsters	56
10. Punishment	58
Rule, Second	66
11. Pod	67
12. Miss Anisha	68
13. Reeducation	72

14.	Compelled	77
15.	Spaces Between	81
16.	Like Clay	83
17.	Hole	88
18.	Blur	91
19.	Greta	92
20.	Lesson Learned	97
	Rule, Third	104
21.	Sounds	105
22.	Fever Dream	107
23.	Into the Deep	115
24.	Strange and Magical	121
25.	Ours is Ours	128
	Epilogue	133
26.	Glossary	137
	Acknowledgements	140
	About Izaic	141
	Afterword - Feeding the Indy Author	143
	Also By	144

When Tall-Men Walk

Legend has it that once in a generation, not so often, when the streets are not too loud, and not too quiet, things walk unseen. Things not quite men, but oh so close, and if you looked with just the right sort of look you might just notice fingers a little too long, eyes a little too deep, and teeth a little too sharp. You see, children, when the streets are just right and the boys and girls without homes are just bad enough, that is when the Tall-Men come. They come to snatch, snatch, and snatch.

They like the thin ones third best, for the crunch of their skin. They like the girl-kind second, for the sweetness of their soul. And they like the magical kind best, for only the Almighty knows what.

Where they take the snatched no one knows, but it's a deep place, and full of magic. That is for sure.

Most are eaten. But sometimes if a child listens just right, the Tall-Men make them their own, turning the snatched into one of them.

-Says Yew Theron, Stroller Extraordinaire

PROLOGUE

Leaving our butterflies with the confused stablemen, I imparted one last message unto the great insects: *Stay and give no trouble. He has the nectar you love so much.* With that last bit, I imparted the taste of the sweet liquid the creature so enjoyed rather than any linguistic representation. The hamlet cut a crisp scent of manure-laced soil, frostbit wood, and musky hearth smoke. My companion and I followed the little girl within the sod-roof house, thankful to finally find reprieve from the blistering winds. I nodded my thanks to the girl, unable to make a sound on account of my missing tongue.

"You have a lovely home," Dirk Ava murmured. Stamping the ice and snow from our boots, we removed our hats and undid our jackets. My hair was the same as ever—black and ageless. Ava's on the other hand had grayed considerably since our first meeting all those years ago. Catching our reflection in a brass-framed, stout mirror, I thought we both looked weary beyond our years. Bounding in a flurry of fur and terrifying howls bolted the girl's dog. The poor child tried to stop the hound but failed miserably. Before the dog could nip at either of us, I touched the back of its neck and urged it to calm down. I had long since come to master my powers, and rarely experienced any animal so strong-willed as to shrug off my suggestions. To the girl's surprise, the dog fell docile, rolling over, and whining when I ceased rubbing the pink of its belly.

"Brutis is never like that. Everyone says we ought to get rid of him, but Mama says he'll keep the bad men away." I grimaced at the mention of my once captors. "He has a way with animals," Ava said. "It's a gift."

"I feed the crows sometimes and they like me well enough," quipped the girl, still amazed by me.

"Perhaps you are gifted too. Maybe one day you can come back to Hasbal for testing."

The girl's eyes became moony, dreaming of things much bigger than her quaint life—then they came back to reality. "I can't go. My family is here, and they need me."

Ava smiled, brittle and sad, surely reminded of the obligations that had long since set the story of her life.

"That is good. There is valor in walking the path given to us. Your family must be proud."

The girl smiled.

"Mama is this way. She doesn't talk much anymore and has a lot more night terrors," said the girl, taking our things. She was a Little, verging on the edge of becoming a Big. *Not her. . . No, she has family.* For how much longer I did not know. I prayed we were not too late. According to the physician she had been in and out of consciousness and they didn't think her passing was all too far off. Once our hats and jackets were stowed, we followed the cherry-haired child through the clustered house. In many ways, it reminded me of her den back then, a pit of discarded things. Opening the backroom door, the girl said, "She was sleeping when I left."

WALKTALL

I wasn't the only one to notice the brave tears in her eyes, though I let Ava wipe them away.

"Do you know how to make tea?" Ava asked.

"Just milk and honey," sniffled the girl.

"That would be wonderful. How about you set a kettle and bring one for all of us?"

"Mama takes only broth now."

"Well, we can still set one aside. Every moment is a new one. Perhaps today is different."

The girl nodded and walked somberly away.

"After you, Mute."

I nodded and grabbed the handle, hesitating before opening the door at last.

The air within was stifling and stagnant. The curtains were drawn so that only the barest trickle of lace thin light filtered in between the moth-eaten cloth. A single lantern kept the worst of the dark gloom at bay—though the sight of it took me to a place I would rather forget. Brushing the artifact, I noticed every dent and ding, every shining and rusting spot, and was reminded of all the Bad Men had done to us—*and still do to us.*

"It's the red plague, alright," Ava said, drawing my gaze to the woman in the bed. Despite her frailty and the festering sores marking her face, there was a remarkable likeness to the girl who had shown us in.

My nose flared at the smell of approaching death and piss. I kicked at the strewing herbs along the floorboards, the purifying smell long gone stale.

Freidis. I thought sadly, taking a damp rag from a nearby bowl and mopping her brow. *How long have I searched for you?*

She did not react to my touch and I knew better than to expect it.

"I'll open the windows," Ava sniffed, "this can't be good for the sick." I caught her by the wrist and gruffed a disapproving noise.

"But it—"

I sat and motioned for her to do the same.

"Fine," Ava sighed, twirling a finger in her hair. "But I doubt your friend is going to wake up anytime soon. You promised answers, Mute. It's been years since you learned your letters and I *want* answers. All of them."

I pursed my lips, my gaze transfixed on Freidis. I watched every shallow rise and fall of her chest. I listened to every rasp of breath raking through her throat. I tasted the despair in the room, though I was not sure if it was mine or hers.

"Mute, please," Ava begged. "You have been there for me since the beginning. Just this once, let me be here for you."

My shoulders rose and then sagged. Pulling at the fringes of my ragged beard, I raised my hand and motioned for the pen and paper. My compeer hissed with delight and ruffled through her things, pulling free the tools that I would require.

WALKTALL

Dragging a little table across the wooden floor, I opened the bottle of ink and smoothed out the papers. There would be much to write, but somehow it only seemed proper to do so in Freidis's presence.

Carefully, without any elegance, I began to write:

This tale begins deep one eve...

ONE DEEP NIGHT

Brun Torvold

Deep, one eve, under the gentle emerald wash of the aurora borealis, commonly known as the Almighty's Breath, trudged a sight for sore eyes. Of course, for the children—each one plucked from the streets, bound, hooded, and shackled by strong hands—it was a forced march, but to their captors, it was unbearably slow. They moved as a ghostly processional, painted in strokes of diffused moonlight, rising fog, and shimmering green. The children traveled in a line—chained to one another's ankles, as their captors strode aside them at regular intervals—lit by the flicker of oil lights.

To the naïve eye, they might have appeared as little more than a band of traveling goblins, led by the looming shadows of their Tall-Men—fairies in hand and mischief near the other. Those who possessed more discerning eyes, however, turned quickly away after witnessing the marching troupe. Bothering the Lord Prime's Junto only brought trouble. Whenever a child slowed beyond allowance or dared cry for a loved one, a swift kick was a sure way to return them to their task; a trek that would last more than a few days, weather permitting, and whisking them from Hasbal's familiar streets to a place from which only whispers escaped.

Hooded as I was, only the gentle rush of the waves reached my ears. I knew the sight they matched well enough. The hunching roll of water, chasing

WALKTALL

curls of white foam and spittle onto a beach of pebbles and driftwood, from which it would recede as finger trails pulled back into the sea to begin again. The air was chill against my skin and for every step that I took my heart seemed to beat eightfold. After what seemed an eternity of a stumbling, groping walk, we came to a halt, and I walked into the back of my compeer.

"Ge' off," growled a boy's voice. He sounded about my age.

"Sorry, I lessknew."

Even something so simple as an apology earned me a swift strike from one of our captors. The blow rattling my head, my ensuing cry bringing another, and another, until I finally understood the point well enough—silence and docility were kings. "That'll teach you," said the man, clicking his cudgel back on his belt. There was a rattling of metal, the creak of wood underfoot, and the nicker of horses. My unasked question was answered: one by one, the same rough hands which had abducted us hours ago, now packed us into wagons like a can of pickled vegetables. I must have been nestled somewhere in the middle because all I could feel about myself were bodies; even worse, all I could smell was the noisome stench that clung to all of us orphans.

Gagging in my hood, I heard a murmur of Tumbleweed Wagons, and my worst suspicions were confirmed—if only I knew then just how wrong I was—the blackcoats had arrested us for our thefts no doubt. It was well known that although the Lord Prime strung up the adults, the great leader never did the same to children—at least not publicly, anyway.

Around me, the air was thick with our misery and tears. To my surprise, I found myself strangely calm in the face of my assured doom. I think it was the shock. I mean, what does it *actually* mean to face the hangman's noose? I know I should have feared it because that is what everyone else did, but when does a ten-year-old ever truly consider their own death? That was the province of the sick and elderly, not young boys. Secretly, I wondered if I would see all my friends again, the ones who disappeared over the years until the *Tvi-Tvi* became a gang of one—me. It had been so long since I had last seen them. They were either dead, conscripted into a Big's gang, or found a way out—for most that usually meant joining the army.

The coachman's voice cracked once before the whip and the horses nickered into a trot. The wagons lurched forth and we were off. At first, the way was rather smooth. Hardly a bounce to speak of. I did not know much of what lay outside the walls of the city, but I had heard that the roads to the east and west were as flush as glass, and nothing like the patchwork of cobblestone that made up the streets back in the city. We rode in silence for a considerable way before someone was brave enough to speak. She asked to pee, and the wagon reigned to a halt. There was the sound of feet crunching as one of the men approached.

"Hold it or spoil yourself, girl" spoke the man, loud enough for everyone to hear. His voice was calm and the tone endearing with a grandfatherly quality, but the words were cruel. When the girl complained yet again, the man sighed and I heard the rattle of keys fitting into a lock. I strained my eyes, trying to see through the hood's material, but dark shapes were the best I could make out. The wagon's doors creaked open, and I could feel the press of bodies against mine as unseen hands searched for the girl. Again, the tingling of metal against metal sounded, followed by the sound of someone departing the wagon. Another man's voice sounded, this one different and far crueler.

WALKTALL

9

"Lessmove or else," commanded the man.

The girl cried out. Someone hit her. She was dragged away. Sounded like a heavy carpet over soil. Strange, the noises one learns when they grow up on the streets.

A shiver soared through the wagon like a sickness to be shared. I had not forgotten the last time I had heard that threat. Just as we were being hustled out of Hasbal's eastern gates, before being hooded, a boy too clever for his own good had managed to slip his binds. Racing for his life the same command had been given with the clarity of a sea hawk's cry. And when the boy did not stop, they placed a piece of lead in him and left him to die. That was when I knew I was really in trouble. For real trouble. The Blackcoats at the gates turned the other way and on we marched to the sounds of the boy's fading cries.

We stayed there for a while more and despite the circumstances, I could not think of much more than the way my right knee ached. It was pushed in at a weird angle at the behest of a larger child's body. Poking them with the side of my knuckle I asked them to move over.

"Shut up," hissed the boy—however, on account of his hood and my hood, the words amounted to something approximating, *"Suthup."*

"Huh? Just move, my knee feels lessgood."

This time the boy responded with a nicely placed pinch to my side. This time I got the point. *How long before we get going? Where are we going?* I privately wondered. *Why is it taking so long? I wish she would hurry up; I am cold.*

A few more whispers enveloped the wagon but they were all put to rest by threats from the Bigs—the nickname for the older orphans caught between childhood and adulthood. Eventually, a set of footsteps returned and the wagon gates were closed and locked. The wagon lurched back to life and we continued on to our destination—wherever that was. I never did learn if that girl was returned to the wagon, though I suspected not. Honestly, I didn't care. My knee hurt, my face was turning chilly from the perspiration trapped by my hood, and my stomach grumbled something fierce. Little did I know that hunger and discomfort were soon to become my only real companions over the four-day journey. The men only stopped once a day to give us the chance to relieve ourselves, and only in small groups of three. Once a night, after the Bad Men set up their camp, we were allowed a single ladle of water and a cup of salty fish broth.

The rules were always the same: "Mosteat and doublelesslook."

The first night I greedily drank the shimmering broth, hoping they would bring seconds, but when the men replaced the hood upon my head all such hopes were dashed. On the second and third nights, I tried to eat slower, but the broth disappeared as swiftly as the first night. On the final night, I had the good sense to finally take a look around once my hood was removed. I saw little else besides my compeers—the night was so dark. They were all as skinny as I, which for orphans was more often the norm than not. Our captors tents blotted out their campfire, giving us only outlines in yellow and orange, and none of the warmth. A tuft of hardy sedge poked me through my trousers, the innocuous little flowers on it's stem rippling in the breeze. The air was free of the salty spray that precipitated the Hasbian streets and there was not a tree in sight. From what I could see we were in a stony desert, which explained the unbroken, cruel, biting winds. It was not a place where even the Almighty would

WALKTALL

show His colors in the sky. With so little to go on it was easier to make a conclusion based on what wasn't there.

Fretfully, I remembered tales of such places while listening to the Strollers that frequented Madam Else and her girls. Every Pax Nomus we orphans would fight tooth and nail—literally and sometimes arriving with a fresh gash or shiner—for the chance to listen beside the fire as the Stroller told their tale. It was from these traveling story-tellers I recognized this place for what it was. A land where fey, fel, and material met. A land between life and death. Where things unholy came and folly went. Craning my head to see behind me I was startled by a pecking sting. First upon my neck and then chest. Looking in the direction of the offense, I saw another boy, gangly of nature and with enough freckles to rival a stormy night. He was the only one who was also brave enough to look up from his broth. A small pebble fell from his hands, and he shook his head. But I was too late in my understanding.

Hands meant for a bear grasped me by my hair and ripped me to my feet. Those nearest gave a shout as they too were knocked about—on account of the chains—and their bowls knocked asunder. Those hands gave me a rough shake as if I were little more than a rug to be beaten clean. The Bad Man leered at me, showering me in spittle, which seemed to accompany the ends of all his words.

"Mostthink you're special?"

"No, no, no no no no!" I stuttered. The only thing special about me was what I could make animals do and *only* on occasion at that.

"Then why are you not doing as told?" he asked, though it was more a command than a question. My hands fumbled as his grasp shifted from my scalp to my neck. I was a fox in a snare. A trap intent on crushing my windpipe and selling my heart. Why else would they take us so far away from the sea and into the land where the Tall-Men played?

"Lessfun when lesslisten, huh?" he laughed, as my eyes widened in panic. My vision shrank and the darkness of the periphery grew fuller and fuller until only a pinprick remained. *This is the end,* I thought, my hands slipping away from his paws to hang listlessly at my side. My feet and fingers tingled and my lungs burned with exertion, but I could not get air past his grasp. The next thing I knew I was being pulled to a seat, this time by orphan hands. They rubbed my back until I was done coughing. I hacked a fit so strong it wouldn't have been surprising if I lost my spleen or something, not that I really knew what it was. One time a Big had threatened to stab me in it if he ever caught me and my short legs around his turf.

"Next time you make a nuisance like the last one, I doublemostpromise the Deep Ones, to un you and piss on your body," said our captor, before stalking away. *Skit!* Now I knew what had happened to that girl.

"There little one," spoke the same comforting voice days before, heard in pockets here and there. "Only the moststrong will survive this journey though most won't." The owner of the voice knelt beside me and gently pressed the bowl back into my hands. Seeing it empty was enough to bring tears to my eyes but they didn't stay long as he gently wiped them away. For how weathered they seemed his hands were remarkably soft. Looking up I saw a man beginning to gray with a face carved from granite, stern and callous, and spotted faintly with liver marks. I knew the look, Madam Else had many Dzhons who also spent plenty of time in the bottle before and

WALKTALL

after rutting upstairs. His clothing cut him a shade lighter than the night and pinched his waist, making him seem more emaciated than us.

"Na, na, na. . ." the man said. "You lesshear me boy? It is a good thing I am here because any other member of this Junto would have uned you as an example for breaking the rules. Look, you have two good eyes when not filled with salt water." Running his hands in the hard soil he worked to upturn the rocky ground. It took him minutes more, but eventually, a satisfied sigh escaped his lips, as he finally worked his way into the richer, damper soil. Scraping just a little more he found what it was that he sought. Wriggling between the pincher of his index and thumb was a thin worm. The poor creature's pale body curled and twisted in vain. Eviscerating it into two he dropped the two halves—still writhing—into the shallow of my bowl.

"There," he said amiably. "There is always a way for those strong enough to find it. You may not understand it now or even ever, but you have been chosen to serve, *if* you can transform yourself into something more. . . more than you ever thought possible."

"Transform?" I asked, my words raw and meek across the flesh of my throat. "I lessunderstand. . ."

"Of course you do. You have seen a butterfly before, yes?"

"Yes," I said, keeping my answers short for fear of saying the wrong thing.

"Ah, ah, ah. . . then ponder that. Ponder that and know there is magic in where we go," he said, drawing to his feet and walking back to their campfire. I did not have much time to think on all that occurred, as my captors had begun their arduous task of hooding us all once again. From my quick glance, we were easily four dozen strong. That was a lot of hoods to put on. Screwing my face up I fished out the worm half and tried to imagine it as warm stuffed bread, rich with cheese and butter. Popping it into my mouth I swallowed faster than my gag reflex could accommodate. I was surprised to find—besides the grit and slime—the taste to be quite manageable. Looking at the hole from which the man had excavated the little creature I made my decision. Digging, until I found more and more to eat. By the time my captors came to hood me, I was slurping and popping everything from roots to worms, to indescribable six-legged things into my mouth.

"Looks like you screwed 'im up worse than you thought, Ghent," said one of the Bad Men, with a mixture of mirth and disgust, joking amongst themselves about my beastly state.

"Just put the rat in the bag."

"Aye, compeer. Supper's over."

A hood descended over my head and enveloped me in it's embrace. It smelt of vomit and stomach acid. *I am all out of luck*. Wrinkling my nose, I hobbled my way back to the wagon without complaint, now more than competent at ambling blindly by the pull of our chains. Packed back into the wagon, knees to my chest, I tried to find sleep, though little came. Instead, this night was dominated by nightmares of that man's eyes. Jewels filled with the gray calm before a storm. Unblinking and all-seeing. On that day, I came to know, to fear, and at times even to worship the one I would call Liverspots.

WELCOME TO VYESGORS

Brun Torvold

Loose soil gives way to the endless clatter of hooves and wagon wheels. As we drew near our final destination the "Ho," of the driver announced the lull in clattering chains, creaking wood, and turning wheels—calm at last from the journey's relentless sways. The smell of my hood is all that I know but I sense that everything has changed. The air is stiff and heavy like a springtide evening before a hanging. Bodies push up against mine in a familiar fashion, learned over the week and a half's journey, one that began in a tamer country. The shout of our captors, the Bad Men, followed by the clacking of their cudgels along the bars of our cage, and the teeth of their keys biting into the lock of the doors. We know the drill now and push into the blind groping vestige of a line. It's not so hard, even if blind. Children learn fast. Besides, we have all stood in the bread lines at one time or another, hungry, and nervous. Were it not for the chain and days of pain it might have even felt familiar. The wagons bid a final creak farewell as our feet slapped the grain of the wood and cold hands hoisted us to the ground. My toes wriggle in rocky soil, frosty to the touch. This place hadn't a sound, not a chewink from a bird, or a whistle from the wind.

"Welcome compeers, to Vyesgors, your new home," Liverspots said, in his peculiar way that allowed a whole room to hear him without hardly raising his voice. "Listen well compeers, for I will lessrepeat myself. The rules here are simple and you shall live so long as you follow them. Rule, first. . ."

We were silent, for everyone knew better than to speak. It was a muting of two parts, one from the threat of the Bad Men and one from a land where silence only escaped.

Rule, First

. . . henceforth all are unnamed.
Those who are doubleplusmostgood
shall be gifted a new name in time.
Those who are lessgood or lessunname
themselves shall be uned. . .
additionally, should any of you leave this
cavern named home,
lessons will mostbegin as obedience will be
revealed mostless. . .

-Says Liverspots to the Children

Hair Harold

Three Soups

Brun Torvold

"What name, compeer?" he asked in the choppy language of our homeland. When I didn't answer, the boy thumbed himself in the chest and spoke louder as if I were hard of hearing. "Hair Harold. That's what I am called." Despite the cavern's dim lighting, I could see just how proud his cherry cheeks shone. He was the sort of child whom others followed, chasing after his antics in an attempt to be just like him. A natural-born leader who, if left on the street, likely would have inherited or started his own gang. I on the other hand was neither shy nor outgoing, I just was. The sort with enough good sense to observe the eddies before diving in.

"Are you deaf?" Hair Harold asked, draining the last of his gruel.

"Na," chirped another, "they beat him a few days in. Broke wha' tween his ears. I've seen him eat bugs and once even crow. Raw!" The youth came closer, free to roam within the confines of this cavern—as we all were, but *only* in this particular cave. He was a gangly boy on the verge of becoming a Big, if not already there, and was as thin as a clothesline. "You mostheard what they said," the boy chirped, swiping supper from my hands. "Only doublemoststrong survive. It is better to let a halfwit un." The boy raised my bowl to drink but was stopped by Harold, whose hand clamped his wrist.

"Ey! Le' go."

"Ja, ja," Hair Harold nodded. "I will, but what was your name first?"

"It's Kim Miroslav, but everyone just calls me Big Oslav," he said.

"Ja, ja," Hair Harold, nodded, releasing him. "I thought I recognized you. You're the *Krasdjeveyy* Prime?"

"Yep bet," Big Oslav said between long draughts of my food. "And I'm putting together a new gang." Once finished he tossed the bowl back in my face and scattered what remained of the contents across my clothes and the floor. I felt my knuckles pop and the teeth grinding in my mouth. I wanted nothing more than to wring his neck. Images of his brain scattered across the ground filled my mind. A child shouldn't have been able to imagine such things, but I once witnessed a Little slip from a rooftop, which naturally ended with a very messy splat.

"Ja, really?" Hair Harold said. He must have noticed the fury boiling within me because just as I made to stand, he stepped between us, and with one hand pushed me onto my rump. The ease at which he handled me was enough to remind me of my short stature; quenching my thirst for retribution in cold embarrassment.

"Ja really," Big Oslav said, mocking Hair Harold's eastern accent.

"That's not funny."

WALKTALL

"Here's the deal, outlander, I decide what's funny. It's the perk of being the Prime."

"But aren't the Bad Men the Prime?"

"This lessdifferent from the streets, compeer. They set the rules and we play the game to mostsurvive. Gangs are strong and alone doublelessstrong. Kiss it and know your Prime," Big Oslav said, shoving his hand into Hair Harold's face.

Gently the boy pushed away the fingers, brown with scum and flecked with whatever else could cake a child's hand. "Ja but lessspeed first."

"Wha' do you lessunderstand?"

"If you have been building a gang, why am I just now hearing it?" He had a point, it had been a while since we arrived at this deep place. Pinpricks of red clouded the back of Big Oslav's neck as he crossed his arms. "Causin you're the first," he sniffed. "You should be doubleplus-mosthonored. You're the next biggest to me, which would make you my right-hand man."

"JA!" Hair Harold exclaimed, his eyes widening in excitement. "That is neat!"

"I know," Big Oslav grinned impishly, "between you and I . . . we could run this place. What do you say?"

"Hmm. . . I say. . ." Hair Harold pondered, making a big show of it. "That I would rather follow a swine painted up like a street lady than you."

"Wha?" But Big Oslav never got a chance to finish the thought before Hair Harold planted a fist right on his kisser. The Big stumbled back, tripping over an unfortunate Little's outstretched legs, and falling headfirst into the ground.

"You hit me! My tooth," he said, spitting a white chomper into his palms. I couldn't help but snicker. The look on Big Oslav's face was priceless. Like a horse's arse if it were crossed with anger and surprise. Oh, and if it had been robbed blind too.

"It'll be lessgood the next time you pick on a halfwit. This one is under my protection."

Scrambling to his feet, Big Oslav said something to the effect of, "You'll regret this", but it was hard to tell between the chorus of giggling orphans and the bloody hand over his mouth. Flushing, he fled. Once the excitement had died down, Hair Harold came to sit by me once again.

"Thank you," I mumbled.

"He does speak," Hair Harold smiled.

"I could have taken care of myself," I whispered, so only he could hear.

"In teasing or begging or even pickpocketing I am sure. . . but in a fight?"

"I can fight," I said hastily. "I didn't need help."

Hair Harold raised a blonde eyebrow and though he shook his head he did little else to dissuade me of the notion.

"Fine," he shrugged at last, "then I'll go."

"Wait, I mean, what do you want from me?"

WALKTALL

"Who said I wanted anything," Hair Harold said with a look of mock hurt. "Is wanting a compeer not enough?"

"I'm not going to be a Painted Boy," I said. "So, if that's it then try someone else."

"Ja, ja, I would not want that on my deepest enemy," he said, so gravely that it disavowed me of any such notion.

"Then what? Nobody wants nothing."

"Ja, ja, ja. You have me out. I too am looking to make a gang and I know you're not crazy as everyone says."

"You don't know that," I tried to firmly say, but instead succeding in only a whiny drawl.

"I know what a survivor looks like. And I know how everyone else sees you. A crazy midget who eats anything and everything. Rumor has it you even poop on yourself to keep the Bad Men away."

"Who says it's a rumor? Maybe I'll shit on you. Need some?" I growled.

"You reek but not *that* bad. Smells like a rumor," he sniffed. "But, if it's true and I am in need then I will call on you."

"You're calling now. What do you want?"

"I want you as the eyes and ears of my gang. People talk freely in front of you, Littles, Bigs, and Bad Men alike. Quiet ones like you can be useful—dangerous even. People talk freely in front of the quiet ones. You can learn things others can't, which is valuable for a gang."

Cocking my head, I looked at him properly for the first time since his intrusion.

"I know you," I gasped.

"Ja, ja, ja," smiled the boy from the campsite—the boy who had thrown the pebbles at me, trying to warn me of the Bad Man.

He was a bold boy, colored ghostly white—even by the standards of a Hasbian. Hair Harold was possessed of hair so fine that the golden threads bordered on the verge of transparency. Most striking of all was a nose broken and twisted so many times that it's crookedness vouched as a resume to his association with conflict. However, it did not answer the most important question of all: How many of those had Hair Harold managed to win?

Considering his offer, I quickly thought it over. After all, everyone without wool for ears knew the benefits of a street gang. Belonging to one might make the difference of whether or not an orphan like me survived, but the cost of entering a gang could also be the same as the price of not: Namely, one's life.

Only one question remained.

"What's my cut gonna be?"

"As First Partner," Hair Harold said, his eyes twinkling, "half of my cut and your life."

"Deal," I said, spitting into my hand and raising it to shake. Hair Harold's face creased in disgust at the yellow bumps of gunk oozing from the wad of phlegm encrusted my palm. His lip curled. "Deal but on account of remaining a halfwit in the minds of others—also I will lessshake that."

"Works for me," I said wiping it upon the front of my shirt.

"So, what is your name?" Harold asked.

"Call me whatever you want, but I ain't saying it," I shrugged. "You heard the first rule."

"Ja," Harold mused, "then Halfwit shall do. Welcome to the *Mal'svoloc*, you will do nicely. . ."

LIGHT GIFTS

Eight Soups

Brun Torvol - H

The bad men warned us that we were neither to speak our names nor depart the confines of our cavern abode—though we were free to walk about unchained. At first, it wasn't so bad. After spending days cooped up in the little wagons, it was a treat to walk freely about. But that feeling didn't last long for me or anyone else; Big or Little, we were all restless children. At first, most of us were afraid, but when the hours rolled by without a sight or sound of the Bad Men we grew more bold; we amused ourselves in trouble and games. Soon the cave echoed with our voices.

In no time at all, Hair Harold had recruited three others to the *Mal'svoloc*. Gleb Peter was a spry Little with a gift for teasing, while Nils Marchovich—or Marco as he often preferred—and Nils Yegor were identical Bigs. The twins had a certain knack for the grim and twisted. Peter and Harold teased me for being too timid to speak and the Nils twins were kind enough to compare me to the dead. "The unned dun talk and that's why nobody messes with them."

At first, I wondered what purpose a gang might actually serve in a place like this. It felt nothing like the streets of Hasbal and yet the game of survival was all the same. Numbers, numbers, numbers. Together even the smallest Little could be mighty, and divided the strongest Big could be as weak as a mouse. I was happy soon enough and contented knowing that Hair Harold saw something in me.

Time dribbled by. Without the sun to guide us, day and night became one. No Bad Men came for what felt like an eternity and without them, there was no food. Just as I thought my belly couldn't handle the gnawing ache any further, bowls of broth were finally delivered. Street children are accustomed to hunger, so for us all to descend upon the food like mad street dogs, should have been my first clue as to how much time had passed. But in the end, it was Harold who pointed it out.

"Look at that," Harold said, pointing at a bulbous oil lantern. Around the cave, a dozen or so similar brass and glass artifacts poured out warm shades of light.

"About a quart of oil left, Prime," Peter said.

"And after that, *kapoof!*" Yegor giggled.

"It goes dark and the Deep Ones come out to play," Marchovich smiled cruelly. I shivered relieved and disturbed to be on the same side as him.

"Ja! Exactly. This is our first score."

"How you mean?" frowned one of the Nils twins.

"Simple Marco, which is complex for you, I know." Harold smiled, smug at his confusion. "Can any of you ninnies tell me why this is so important? Well, except for Halfwit, 'cause you're just a halfwit and all."

My cheeks flushed and my shoulders nearly rose to my ears, but I relaxed after a merry wink from the Big. I nearly forgot that I was playing the role of a halfwit, not that I actually was, though sometimes the insults stung all the same. My role, as Harold had made keenly clear, was to be a Little that others would have no problem speaking in front of. It really was no different than teasing a mark. Sometimes you had to pretend to be the unfortunate victim of an accident, other times a begging invalid, and occasionally a fast-talking trickster; in the end, all elements of a good tease required just enough importance to play the part and never be remembered. Who my marks were, I had no idea, I was more worried about how Harold was going to get us more food. In response to my thoughts, my stomach growled fiercely enough to startle my compeers.

"Ja, ja. I know Halfwit, I am trying to get your aching belly filled, eh? Back to lights, what makes them important?"

The twins looked at one another and then down at their feet.

"Causin the brass is worth a gift?" Peter asked hopefully.

"Na, na, na," Harold said, crossing his arms and dashing the smile from Peter's face. "It's because there is *only* a quart of oil left in there. Listen, all these lanterns were burning when they dumped us off, and once they burn off then—"

"*Kapoof!*" Yegor exclaimed.

"Ja. Exactly it gets darker than the crescent of ladies, you know."

WALKTALL

Peter frowned and raised his hand.

"But they'll just replace the oil when it runs out. I dun see how these could be a score, Prime?"

"Compeer, what do you smell?"

We all took a whiff. I don't know what the other *Mal'svoloc's* smelled but I thought it to be a unique mix of dust and shit, combined with the musky sweat of dried terror and mushed crowberries—of the latter, I only knew the smell on account of getting ripping drunk on a stolen pitcher of the stuff.

"Uh, smells like poopoo," Peter hesitated, clearly anxious to get something right.

"Ja, ja, ja!" Harold beamed casting the Little a proper salute. "They don't clean our shit, they don't deliver the food except leaving it at the entry, and they never take our dishes. The cods are avoiding us for some reason which makes these. . ."

"The reason they are lesscoming," Yegor said.

"Na, na, na," Harold growled, shaking his head. "I'm beginning to wonder who the actual *halfwits* are here. It means light is scarce *because* they ain't been refilling em *and* that makes it a gift. Our first score is to nab all of them, then pour all the oil into a few and take control of the light. If any of these piss-wads want to see their hands, they will be begging to be near us, and for that, we will charge a gift from each. One-fourth a bowl of their soups should do. Not much to them, but a whole lot for us."

Excitement bubbled across the *Mal'svolocs*. The Nils twins flashed wicked grins, and Peter sucked up to his Prime—naming him "bold" and "clever."

"Enough, enough, enough. Get to work and get lesscaught. Na, not you Halfwit. Here, come this way. . ." Harold led me away from the others, well out of earshot. "That work is too intelligent for you. Why don't you get a lay of the land and see if there is anyone else worth joining our little crew? We got room for one more and I want 'em to be good."

"And if they're lessgood?"

Harold crossed his arms, the starts of what would one day be a golden forest of forearm hair, glinting in the light.

"Do your best."

Nodding, I wandered back into the sea of children, well, maybe a pond of children. I didn't pay much attention. Faces. I passed lots of faces. Most dispirited after what had likely been days of this horrid treatment. They all either ignored me or swatted me away—sometimes gently but most were violent. Thankfully the Almighty had blessed me with a talent for being nimble and I avoided the worst of the abuses thrown my way. Leaving the crowd, I took the hint, and left to explore the rest of our cavernous home; I was smart enough to know where not to go—mostly.

In the far back right, where the rock rose from floor and ceiling like the teeth of a whale shark—or at least what I imagined they should look like—was the fanged nest of the *Krasinya*, our one and only rival gang. From behind those foreboding gates of rock, Big Oslav and his little mob of cretins were certainly plotting how to get back at Hair Harold, and by extension, me. Tucking my head, I left the miasma of children and

WALKTALL

wandered the peripheries of the crowd, unseen and unheard. I had a certain gift for becoming near invisible when I wished it. I just didn't have one of those memorable faces—the kind heroes have.

Nothing and nobody stood out to me, but I also had no idea what qualities Hair Harold was looking for exactly. It seemed to me, that between the *Mal'svoloc* and the *Krasinya*, the Littles and Bigs who made the best recruits were already taken. Everyone else was either too small to play a role, scared half-to-death, or were wasting away. Every wintertide saw orphans die and I knew the look: Eyes that did far too little looking, bodies run thin, and shaking with the pale hope that the next meal, warmth, or whatever might just be enough.

Pursing my lips, I grinned a halfwits smile to a boy whom I had been caught staring at for far too long. I mumbled some nonsense to add to the disguise. It was an easy tease, especially when you meet as many people as I have with split-mind, lunacy, or possession—the crazy one also live on the streets. The boy's fist relaxed and he tugged at his compeer's collar and pointed at me. Their faces paled and they hurried away. The teasing had its proper effect. Everyone knew sicknesses of the psyche could jump from the afflicted to the healthy if one got too close.

Wandering over to the side of a pointy stone, I undid the draw of my pants and proceeded to relieve myself upon it. I nearly fell over as a girl rose up from behind the rock, a darting shadow at first, quickly revealed to be a short Big—or perhaps towering Little. She had eyes as brown as good soil. Her youth was firmed by the stoniness of her features and a tongue sharp as a knife.

"Pissing? I'm surprised it doesn't all just pour out of that. It's so small. Lessmind, that your thumb? Deep Ones, where is it coming from then?" she asked.

The back of my neck prickled bright red, but not because I knew why I should be upset, but because of the way she said it.

"What are you doing where I'm peeing?" I asked hotly.

"Mostsorry *Lord Prime*," the girl bowed. "I didn't realize this cave was all yours." Sniffing she looked me up and down. "I was taking care of things only a lady knows about."

Frowning, I couldn't help but notice the puffy bags beneath her eyes, nor the light blots of blood at the hem of her skirt.

"Wait," I said stuffing everything back into place and pulling the string of my trousers tight again. "Are you hurt? That's blood—"

"Yes, it is," she said distantly as if drifting into a land of dreams, her voice soft and eyes wide. Twitching, her gaze returned to what I assumed was its usual intensity. "And it's none of your business. The next time you pull out your pecker in eyeshot of a lady I promise it will be your last time holding it ever again."

"I'd like to see you try," I said sticking out my tongue.

"You would never see it coming," she said, returning the gesture. "Now, I'm trying to get outta here, so piss off Little. I ain't no street lady."

She's perfect, I thought, *the exact sort of recruit that Harold would want for the Mal'svoloc.* At least I assumed on account of the Big never quite giving

WALKTALL

me specifics. For some reason, this girl felt right. Maybe it was just because she had a scowl that could scour a pot.

"What's your name?" I asked.

"Rut off," she scowled, before disappearing behind the pointy rock once more.

"Fine, Rutoff it is," I called to no response. Part of me wanted to follow her and invite her to join our gang, but she—like everyone else—was bigger than me. I also believed that cutting off my pecker was the least of the things she might do to me. No, when the world is twice your size, you learn to navigate it as a mouse and sometimes as a rat. *Let Harold talk to her,* I decided. Shoving my hands into the greasy folds of my pockets, I wandered back to *Mal'svoloc* territory—where a gathering array of flickering lights was beginning to accumulate.

Blood Money

Fourteen Soups

Brun Torvo - Hal

"I swear it's less, Prime," Peter said, licking the last drops of grease-free of his fingernails. The five of us sat around our lamps, eating like the little kings we were. The tips of our fingers and the rims of our lips had waxy glisten under the flickering light. "Ja," Harold said, his usual smile undeterred despite our general lack of spirit. "That's obvious. But look, thanks to this little score of ours *we* have more than enough." The Nils twins cackled, slurping up the last dredges of soup from their bowls. I, on the other hand, had learned to prolong my meals and thus only sipped the salty liquid. Hair Harold's plan was working brilliantly. To bask in our lamplight, the other orphans paid us tribute, and in turn, were not forced into the outer darkness. The Nils twins swiftly crushed any and all challenges to our reign. Again, I found myself thankful to have them on our side. Still, when I looked at all the other orphans, I couldn't help but feel something for them. They were all so hungry and we took what little they had.

Four soups ago, a Big had come down with a fever and shakes; he'd all but begged us for some of our extra food. Unable to help myself, I'd made to give him a little of what I had but was stopped by Harold.

WALKTALL

35

"Ours is ours and theirs is mostours," he said, reciting the *Mal'svoloc* creed.

I thought I would never forget the boy but when he passed six soups later—I think, maybe it was only three soups—his face had already slipped my mind.

"For true," Peter said, turning my thoughts from the recent past and back to the present. Per usual the Little was in the midst of sucking up to Harold. "It's cause your doubleplussmart."

"Ja, ja." Harold rolled his eyes, accepting the last offering of soup for the "day".

"We have so much we could probably even share."

"Ours is ours and theirs is *mostours*," I said, flicking a pebble into the darkness—the words felt hollow but the belonging they induced did not.

The *Mal'svoloc* paused—save Harold—and all turned to face me wide-eyed. It was the Nils twins who finally broke the silence.

"Halfwit can speak proper," Marchovich grinned, all teeth.

I flushed, my eyes darting to Harold, afraid to have let him down. But instead of becoming angry, his smile broadened. "I said he was a halfwit, not mute."

"Das true," Peter quipped.

Nils Yegor giggled, muttering something about how stupid his brother was.

And so some variation of that was how our "days" went from there on.

We continued to measure the passage of time by the soups we received, which always seemed to come at random. Every time they came we collected our tribute and so it was. Everyone in the cavern grew steadily malnourished—though the *Mal'svoloc* less so—and soon enough the sick and dying became a normal part of life. Strange things happened too. Some of the children had curious dreams. Said they saw ghosts and stuff. Some even said the ghosts wanted them to follow, to help them escape. That scared me and I tried to erase those stories from my mind.

We found dumb games to pass the time, fought the *Krasinya* whenever they got out of line, and one time I even went to find the girl from before—Rutoff. Mysteriously, she had all but vanished, though I did find something interesting behind the pointy rock where we had met. Wandering around, I nearly fell into a sloped depression that fed into the mouth of a hole in the cavern floor. I could barely see into the chimney, for it was so edged in shadows of sable and grey, but I knew well enough it only led further into the deep. This was no way out and only a crazy person would dare descend within it. Rutoff, as sad as it was to admit, was very likely dead. Just another orphan, gone.

The only time our captors ever truly entered the cavern was to collect the dead. On such occasions, they were always armed to the teeth, which was unnecessary as we had long since learned not to resist them. Once, Liverspots even accompanied the men, dressed in his flowing robes and the tallest *ushanka* that I had ever seen. Grinning, he examined our little racquet and left just as he came—without a word. Still, that look was one I could not forget. It was the kind of look one has when they know the fighting cock they'd bet against was about to die. I wasn't the only one Liverspots seemed to bother, Harold said as much.

WALKTALL

"He likes you," Harold said one time, placing a hand on my shoulder.

"Me?"

"Ja. I dunno why, but if we're gonna get outa here, I think you're gonna be the key, Halfwit."

"I lessknow that."

"I doubleplusknow that look," Harold said with a pained stare. I could tell something bothered him but I had no idea what it could be. "Never mind, you'll be fine." Harold left to stoop between the Nils twins, who were currently playing dice with a rock they'd found—how the game worked, or what the sides of the rock meant made no sense.

I Believe In Magic

Fifteen soups

Brun Tor- Hal

The Nils twins delighted in their cruel game. The poor bat screamed. The screech echoed across through the cave and past the dirty clusters of children. I was torn from my bored contemplation at the edges of our territory—I had been listening to yet another cry of nightmares from some unseen child. Something about ghosts or another. I didn't care. The bat screamed again. Sprinting, I leaped over the flat slab that served as the center of our operations. My little legs carried me through the indents where we huddled for warmth at night. The panicked squeals were louder and more frequent now.

I'm coming!

The twin's backs were to me as I approached. They giggled amongst themselves; the bats fluttering form caught in their hands.

"Little squeezes," Yegor said to his brother. "Make it lessfast."

"Get off my back, Yegor," Marchovich whined. "I know how to do it."

WALKTALL

"Yea, but your nails! You're drawing blood, Marco. It's all about the crushing. They scream more!"

"Would you shut up about it? You got the cat outside of Old Man Anya's, now it's *my turn*. I bet this is gonna taste so, so, so doubleplusgood! We're not sharing, right?"

Yegor never got a chance to answer. I crashed into them. My sudden shoving arrival stopped them dumb. Snatching the poor thing I pulled it close to my heart. The bat fluttered, trying to get away, screeching and clicking. I winced as its claws slashed the inside of my palms.

I'm trying to save you! Calm! Calm! I tried to use my powers—to imprint my will upon the creature. Sometimes it worked and other times it didn't. I sighed in relief as the animal stilled. I wasn't in the clear yet, however. Just barely ducking a fist, I scurried away from the twins. The Nils dogged my steps, fury on their faces and venom in their words.

"Give it back, Halfwit!"

"If you dun I'll pummel the other wit outta you!"

"Harold and Peter are away. No one is here to protect you, Halfwit."

I squealed, my short legs only able to keep my pursuers away for so long. Marchovich snatched me by the scruff of my neck and his brother was winding up to hit me.

"Bat! Bat!" I frantically pleaded. "Hit me and you'll hit it!"

Yegor paused and looked at his brother. He shrugged and smiled, hitting me all the same.

The poor animal didn't stand a chance. It fell lifeless in my grip. His punch crunched every bone in its body and nailed me in the stomach. I crumpled into a crying, infantile mess. Someone kicked me twice, or maybe each kicked me once—it didn't matter.

"Lessmess with us again," Yegor snarled into my ear. "I dun why Harold keeps you around but give us a gift and go un yourself, weakling."

"But ours is ours," I whimpered.

"*Ours* is *ours*," Marchovich said, extracting the dead bat from my hands. "You do nothing for us. *Yours is ours.* Come on, Yegor. We can still eat it least." They walked away, leaving me in tears. I don't know how long I was there before Peter and Harold found me. It could have been minutes or hours.

"What happened?" Harold asked, pulling me up as Peter dusted me off.

By this time, the waiver in my voice had fallen even, but my words were hoarse and hard to hear. I told them what had happened. Harold stiffened, his eyes narrowing, and knuckles popping. Silently, he thought it over and then spoke, deliberately and slowly.

"Peter, take care of him, ja? I'm gonna go have a talk with the others."

Peter saluted.

"You alright?" Peter asked, helping me to my feet, and guiding me to the edge of our territory. I nodded. Suddenly, I was *very* alright. Harold's shift from warm to icy wrath was enough to end my tears.

WALKTALL   41

"You should have lessbothered them," Peter said, sitting me down and using his grubby shirt to clean my dirty face. There was a howl. Harold was hitting the twins. I felt a pang of guilt. I knew I shouldn't.

"Dun think about it," Peter said. "Punishment is punishment."

"I just wanted to help it," I said.

"The bat?"

"What? Why? It's just a filthy animal."

I didn't point out that we were also disgusting.

"No reason," I sniffed, looking at my feet.

"Come on, Halfwit," Peter said. "You can tell me. Us Littles have to stick together."

"It's stupid," I said. After all, that's what everyone said when I told them about my peculiar powers—why should Peter be any different?

"Try me."

Looking him up and down, I nodded. I don't know why, maybe it was because we were Littles, or maybe it was because he had always been kind to me. "I can talk with animals, Peter. Sort of, anyway." I expected him to laugh, to jeer, to tell me I really was a halfwit, but he did none of those things. Instead, Peter nodded, deadly serious.

"I see."

"You believe me?" I blinked in surprise.

"I dun see why I lesshould?"

"Because it sounds *crazy*!"

He shrugged. "I once saw a man fly."

"You did?" Now it was my turn for disbelief.

"Yes! I also once heard of a man who stole a star, kissed life into a unned woman, and spoke the sea to sleep. Of course I believe in magic!"

I almost laughed and I would have, if not for the conviction on his face. I didn't tell him I'd also heard the Strollers tell the story of *Unni and the Three Wonders*. I also didn't remind him that Unni had a hat that could make him appear however he wished. I just smiled.

"What did you want to do with the bat?" Peter asked.

"Help it," I shrugged.

"That would have been nice."

"I wish someone would help us," I said.

Peter's eyes glazed slightly as if looking through frosted glass, and his body tensed against mine. "That would have been most nice," he repeated. Then he licked his lips. "Still, I bet it tasted good though. Better than fish broth. I wish I could have helped it *and* tried it."

I nodded, although wishing only that I had helped the poor thing. It never crossed my mind that I should have asked it to fly away and show me out of the wretched place. I probably could have snuck past the Bad Men if I knew where I was going.

WALKTALL

Marchovich or Yegor, or maybe both, cried out again. I hoped they would be nicer to me. I hoped they wouldn't be mad at me for snitching on them. Secretly, I also enjoyed the heavy tears on the edge of their cries.

COMMON LANGUAGE

Seventeen soups

Brun To- Half

Some things make no sense, such as a heavy purse, a roof overhead, or clothes without patches—fighting on the other hand made perfect sense. I was pretty sure that was how the Nils Twins felt about it. For what felt like the hundredth time, I watched as Harold and the twins protected our turf from the *Krasinya*. Like all fights, this one took place on the ground, scuffling scrawny bodies scraping across the stone. Saliva and blood left blots in the dirt and speckled upon their bodies. The first few times our gangs had gone at it, the other orphans had cheered it on, excited at the prospect of a diversion, but this time we were the only ones who cared. For my part, I hung back, staying well away from the action.

"Skat!" screamed one of the boys.

"You picked it," Yegor growled coming up for air. Smiling like a madman, his teeth yellow, white, and pink. Howling the boy tried to free himself from the Big but Yegor held him fast, biting into his scalp once again. Beside him, Marchovich was in the midst of fighting a different Big. The twin

WALKTALL

was currently using a particularly sharp stone to try and stab him—which he did.

"Deep Ones!" howled the *Krasinya* Big. I cheered as Marcovich scored a fat fist across the boy's jaw, dropping him to the ground. Kicking him in the face, the twin laughed cruelly when the boy's eyes rolled into the back of his head, nose crunching from the force. All the while, Harold and Big Oslav went at it. Despite Big Oslav's advantage in size, Harold was the superior fighter. Unfortunately for Harold, Big Oslav never brawled fairly. Two Littles fought like angry eels at his side, both "biting" at Harold whenever he seemed to gain the upper hand.

"It's against the code to bring Littles into a fight, coward!"

"That's street gangs. Does this look like a pissing street to you?" Big Oslav spat.

Tense words volleyed back and forth, but ultimately the sound of most was lost in the collision of their bodies. Fists struck flesh, drawing blood, leaving marks sallow with bruising, and sending teeth flying. As usual, we were gaining the upper hand. It wouldn't be long before the *Krasinya* tucked tail and ran. Pulling my legs up to my chest, I pushed myself into the little cubby of rock I called my own. I watched as the Nils, who had managed to get the better of one of their adversaries, were now toying with the last *Krasinya* Big. Yegor had the raven-haired boy by the arms as Marchovich stoned him once, twice, and thrice. Releasing him, the twins clasped arms and bumped foreheads as the boy staggered into darkness crying for his ma. Peter, braver than I, jumped into the fray wailing like a wild man all the way. The *Krasinya* Littles was so busy harassing Harold, that Peter's target never stood a chance. Snatching him by the scruff of his neck, Peter bit into him, tearing free a chunk.

"Did you see that?" Peter grinned, letting the meat fall from his mouth.

I never knew lips could get so pink without make-up.

"Ja! Now get outa here, idiot."

"But I—"

"Skat and piss on me!" Big Oslav said kneeling over his fallen Little. Slapping the whip-thin boy upon the face, Big Oslav tried to wake him, but his efforts only earned him a single and violent spasm. As sudden as that the fight was over. Like flies drawn to food, we all formed a circle about the two.

Blood. So much blood. Crimson streaks gushed into a delta river that ran down the valley of the Little's neck and pooled into a dark blot upon his threadbare shirt. I was glad it wasn't my first time seeing something like this, but I think it was Peter's.

"You did this," Big Oslav said, leveling a finger at the scrawny boy. "I will un you! I swear it! By the Almighty's bones, I will sarding wear your skin by the day's end."

"I didn't mean to," Peter fumbled, wide-eyed and white as a sheet. "I just wanted to fight too."

"You *uned* him you sarding, deep skat—"

"Ja, ja, ja!" Harold shouted, pushing Big Oslav. "You broke the code first! You should have never had a Little in a gang fight to begin with. Take your dead and leave us be. Ja?"

Grinding his jaw, back and forth, back and forth, Big Oslav finally nodded.

WALKTALL

47

"Janis, take him back to our turf." Stepping timidly between the two, baldheaded Janis retrieved his fallen compeer and retreated eagerly away.

"Good choice," Harold said tersely. Snapping his fingers, he called for the twins.

"What do you need, Prime?" Yegor asked.

"Fill a lamp with a bit of oil and give it to Big Oslav. A peace offering," Harold said, never breaking eye contact with the *Krasinya* Prime.

"But—"

"Do I need to say it again?"

"Uh, na, na. . ." Yegor said, leaving to fulfill the task, grumbling all the way.

In the time that it took to prepare the lantern, light it, and return with it in hand, Big Oslav never moved. Were he not breathing I might have thought him carved of stone. Silently, I wondered if those stories about the Medusa were real. . .

"Here," Yegor said, handing over the lantern. Like a fairy illuminating the truth, the flame revealed the previously hidden features of Big Oslav's face. Crag ridges, once thick with ample reserves of flesh, were now drawn tight against the bone. Once bold eyes now shimmered with the simmer of rage in sunken sockets, above them a thin cut crowned his brow. Grasping the lantern, Big Oslav turned to leave, but unexpectedly rocked back, and slammed it into poor Yegors's head. Glass sprinkled across the ground and the flame was extinguished. Falling to the ground Yegor cradled his face wailing amidst the rising chorus of our commotion.

"Brother!" Marchovich yelled, "Im'a un him! Im'a do it."

"Na, na, na!" Harold snarled, catching the twin between his arms. Harold was just able to hold the twin back, the veins in his hands popping from the exertion.

"That'll do for even. For now," Big Oslav said. Turning to leave he all but melted into the shades of the cavern, now drawn darker with one less lantern. So he went, limping all the way.

"Marco? Oh! Marco, this is it for me! I can see the light. I think the Valkyries are coming for me, Marco."

"Get off me," Marchovich said, slipping loose of Harold's grip. Rushing to his brother's side he rolled him over him for all to see. It was a gruesome sight. Glass shards speckled his face, drawing a net of ruby red to the surface of his skin. Most curious of all was the milky tone that fogged, his once frisco eye. Without thinking, I pulled the shard free of the eyeball. Now that was the worst scream I had ever heard. It was worse than a street lady taking the letting potion.

"Get away, Halfwit!" Marco said, punching me in the chest. The air fled from my lungs and I felt my ribs crackle under the pressure. Falling to the ground, I scrabbled back, afraid that there might be more—thankfully, none came. Perhaps on account of Harold stepping over me and saying, "Halfwit never did anything. He was just trying to help, idiot. Skat, skat, skat. Tie this around that eye. He won't be using it ever again."

"I'm unning," Yegor wailed, only to be slapped by his brother.

"Ah shuddup. It's just your stupid eye! Your lessgood one too, eh? It's the same one that makes the ladies run for the hills. You look better this way."

WALKTALL

49

"You actually think so, Marco?" he asked, once the strip of cloth was bound about the wound.

"Uh, ya," Marchovich said. He wasn't the only one to tilt his head uncertainly.

"Ja, ja," Harold said, helping him to his feet. Yegor wavered uncertainly before being guided away by the Prime. "We won the day compeers! And Yegor here has a scar to remember it by. To us go the spoils and gifts! *Mal'svoloc* for life!"

"*Mal'svoloc* for life," we echoed, some more enthusiastic than others, but proudly all the same. At the end of the day, we were a part of something special, and together it seemed that not even our captors could keep us down.

I wish that had been true.

STILL BOYS

Eighteen soups

Brun To- Half

Following our brawl, some soups later, life eventually returned to normal within the cave. Our gang had taken to the usual schedule of working, watching, and sleeping in shifts; we remained vigilant for the next sign of trouble, trying to find any shred of rest or enjoyment that we could along the way. When it came to sleep, Harold decided it best for some to keep watch. He divided us into groups that would relieve one another after an allotted amount of time, which only Harold seemed to know. Me and Peter formed one shift, while Harold and the brothers formed the other. Anyone on watch was supposed to remain vigilant and undistracted, but me and Peter had taken to playing games in secret. At first, I worried about revealing too much of my intellect during our competitions, and thereby accidentally squashing my status as a halfwit, but the temptation of fun proved too strong to resist. Peter proved to be a good friend, the kind who kept your secrets.

"That's good!" Peter said, smacking his head in disbelief. I smiled. I wasn't just good at knucklebones, I was an expert at the game. "Right, five for ya

WALKTALL   51

and my go." Scooping up the bones from a dead rat, Peter gave the greasy things a fine shake before casting them into the air.

"Go, go, go," I said, unable to help myself. Lips twisted, Peter scooped up as many of our marbles—special rocks we'd found—before the last bone clattered to the ground.

"Five," Peter smiled, counting off our rocks. He said it slow. Really slow. Numbers were not his strong suit. "Dun think I'd match ya, huh? Know what that means?"

"Course I do," I said, perhaps a tad too quickly. A halfwit shouldn't speak so swiftly or surely. Peter looked at me and we both looked at the others. Nearby, Harold's side rose and fell with the drift of his dreaming mind. Not far from him snored the twins, snuggled close for warmth. Nils Marchovich grumbled, but he always did that in his sleep—sometimes even talking. I looked back at Peter and frowned.

"We should probably keep watch," I said, eyeing the *Krasinya's* side of the cave.

"You're supposed to be a halfwit." Peter whispered. He frowned. "Why do you lesstell the others? Our gang is safe."

"I am a good teaser. I live my tease until its done. That's what it means to be a good teaser." I shrugged, gathering the stones and bones. "Besides, Harold told me not to."

"So why dun you tease me?"

"Cause were playing bones," I said hotly. "It's different. This is mostimportant."

Peter didn't argue but he did smile which irritated me all the more.

"I'm the doubleplusbest at this game," Peter said.

"As if."

Shaking my head, I inhaled and tossed the bones.

My hand was a blur, gathering stones like no other. The bones clattered to the side. Placing the stones down, one by one, I reveled in my compeer's groans. Sticking my tongue out with a waggle, I delighted in hearing him count to seven.

"Beat that," I said, well aware that neither of us had ever collected more.

"*Phaw!*" Peter said, sticking out his chest. That was short for, *I dun know if I can.* We were boys and our years were far shorter than the measure of our bravado, so of course Peter assured me he would get twenty before the end of the watch. So we played and bragged and talked. It was the only time that either of us could be just what we were. . . boys.

"You wanna know what I miss?"

"What's dat?" Peter asked, clacking the bones together.

"My flute," I said.

"Ugh, that's for girl-folk. What are you? A pansy?"

"What? No! I hardly knew how to play it." That wasn't true. . . I had stolen it three years ago and taught myself to play, but the rest was true. . . "I used to sit on this nasty witch's home and screech the worst tunes. She'd get so mad, she'd think it was her neighbor and yell at him until they were both green in the face." I smiled. Peter laughed.

WALKTALL

53

"What did she do to you in the first place?"

I shrugged.

"Come on, tell me. Were compeers, right?"

"Fine. . . she was just mean. We lived near her place and every time she saw me, she said lessgood things."

Peter raised an eyebrow. "Sounds like she deserved dat. Wanna know what I miss most?"

"What?"

"My favorite shirt. It was tan with red trim, just like in the army."

"Do you want to join," I frowned, watching him count out the stones collected from his last toss. Four, nothing spectacular.

"Why not? If I make it to being a Big then it's three meals a day. A roof. . ." We both paused, listening to the coughs and quiet cries, reverberant in the cave. We tried to ignore it. We had an unspoken rule for these rare times of boyhood, and it was never to acknowledge that which was around us. Better to live in the moment than fear the future.

"Well, wanna know what I miss more than that?" I asked, tossing the bones.

"What's dat?"

"My squirrel."

Peter scoffed, a gagging sort of noise. "You had a squirrel?"

"Doublemost I did."

"Lesstruth, lesstruth," Peter tutted, nearly sing-song.

"It's true," I said, pushing him.

"You swear?"

"I swear."

"Swear on your heart as a *Mal'svoloc*!"

"I swear," I growled.

"On fear of losing your tongue and being chained to the Deep?"

"I swear, I swear, *I swear!*" At my exclamation the Nil's twins snorted and coughed, turning and twisting. We both froze. We couldn't be caught playing our little game, and I shouldn't be caught as anything more than a simpleton. We held our breath until they snored back into a restful stupor. Peter smiled and said, "Alright. I believe ya. How'd ya get a squirrel?"

I shrugged. "Just got a way with animals, I suppose." Peter narrowed his eyes, giving me an almost stern look, and just when I thought he might object he simply said, "Neat. Your magic, then?"

"Yea, I guess," I said. "I just worry he might think I finally went out to sea. That's my dream, you know. To go somewhere far, far away. . . We used to talk a lot about it—"

"You wanna know what I miss most," Peter interrupted.

"Sure," I said. "That's three this time, by the way." Peter spat and grumbled.

"Anyways," Peter said, "as I was sayin. What I miss most is my bed."

"Oh yeah?" I asked, imagining one of those big special beds people talked about. The kind with posts that reached for the ceiling and were carved with stupid, fancy things.

"Yeah," Peter said dreamily, "it wasn't much, but it was mine. . ." we both trailed off, thinking of our old lives. That was then and this was now. I looked across the shadowy cave at the misery-mired children that still remained. Peter gave a glum glance. "That's why I want to be like Harold when I'm a Big. He knows how to get the best out of life. We gotta stick close to him if we're ever gonna learn. Come on, your turn!"

Shoving all other thoughts away, I blew on the bones for luck, then gave them a great big toss. Frantically I scrabbled after our "marbles". *Six, seven, eight! Eight! I got eight!* I leaped for joy, only to trip in a pothole and lose all but two of my rocks. Chuckling at my expense, Peter delighted in my bad luck. I had eight only a moment before but now to my chagrin, I held only two.

"Two, two, two," Peter sang, taking the bones in hand. "That is the *most-lessgood* turn in the history of *ever*."

I groaned, a sneaking grin turning up the edges of my lip. *I'll show you,* I thought. So we played, and talked, and jeered. These moments were fleeting but as good as gold. It was always good to remember what I was. A boy, before the *Mal'svoloc* or anything else.

JEALOUS MONSTERS

Twenty-Three soups

Brun - Halfwi

True as the darkness of our eternal night, or day if one preferred, the gnawing creep of the hunger finally wound its way into the *Mal'svoloc*. Our soup toll was no longer enough to satisfy the ache in our stomachs, and to make matters worse our ability to exert influence waned as the oil in our lamps was slowly consumed by its greedy flame. The cavern became one great miasma of agony as we all slowly turned from humans to beasts. Fights, not only amongst us and the *Krasinya*, but for all became the rule of law. Blood was drawn over everything, from food to shoes. We were jealous monsters, slaves to our desires, shackled by the needs of the flesh. Every meal and between, it seemed that another one of us died of privation. Beyond the bounds of our lights, whispers of children who ate the flesh of the fallen rode on the curtails of the meek cavern breeze. I may have been a halfwit, but I was smart enough to no longer relieve myself beyond the edges of the light anymore.

Sometime between this soup and that, Hair Harold and I watched as that last vestige of lamplight consumed its final draught of oil. Like a star

WALKTALL

snuffed from the sky, that twinkling light was there one moment and gone the next.

"Skat," was all I said.

"Ja" was all Harold said.

As the cavern dipped into that inky darkness, I wondered whether Harold was as scared as me.

Chaos ensued, for that last light was the only thing keeping most of us sane. It started with a wail and then the madness of the crowd. Frenzying with fright, some of the children ran, and one even bolted for the exit. The idiot left the cave and the first rule was completely shattered.

PUNISHMENT

Twenty-Three soups

Brun -Halfwi

Someone hit me, knocking me down, and my bowl shattered beneath my body. I screamed at the loss. Shoving the kid away, I scrabbled blindly to my feet, swinging all the way. My fist connected with something soft, then air, then something soft. "Idiot! Skatting idiot!" Those were the only words I could muster, which couldn't even begin to explain the cauldron of emotions that I felt. First, a fear of a dark so deep it could paralyze. Then, shreds of anger, burning white hot at the loss of my one and only possession, and last;y, sorrow for my pitiful life. The child in me heard the Tall-Men approaching, but the street orphan knew it was the Bad Men—the wicked men who had snatched us from our old haunts. Children, veiled in the inky coal shadows, ran every which way, pushing, crushing, tripping, fleeing, yelling. The knots of hunger in my belly seemed to tighten under the sable spread and I too lost control.

Chaos. That is all we had left, though that isn't what I called it. Living on the streets taught us some very important lessons, and this one I knew all too well. Everyone is only a few days removed from becoming a beast. Everyone has a breaking point. And we, the survivors, had finally hit ours.

WALKTALL

I fell to the ground. Hard. Shoved there by someone and trampled by another. Sensation, sharp as knives ran the length of my arm. It was wet. I was bleeding. Curling into a ball I breathed: in out, in out, in out, in out, inout inout inout inoutinoutinout. My head rushed and my chest shuddered as it all bled into one inhalation and exhalation. Stars pinged white at the edges of my vision. Vision? What vision? It was so dark, how could there be vision? I was dead and the Tall-Men had gotten me—likely already storing me in their bellies to forever rot.

"Halfwit? Halfwit!"

The voice was familiar. Harold called again. Strong and masculine, tinged with the accent of a warrior. I knew it. I followed it.

"Halfwit! To the *Mal'svolocs*! Follow my voice!"

I followed it and miraculously found my way to its owner. Familiar hands pulled me close. My breathing slowed, though not all the way, but enough to help me calm.

"I got 'em, Prime!" shouted Yegor over the commotion.

"Ja! That's mostgood. We stick together. *Mal'svoloc* for life!"

"*Mal'svoloc* for life!"

They were all there. Peter, Marchovich, Yegor, and Harold. My only family in this horrid nightmare. I should've felt thankful, but all I could think about was the sting in my arm and the loss of my bowl.

"Ya alright, Halfwit?" Peter asked.

"They broke my bowl."

IZAIC YORKS

"Who?" Yegor said.

"I dunno," I moaned.

"Bastards," Marchovich snarled. "I'll wring that little chicken's neck, they won't ever take a step near you again."

"And just how are you gonna sarding do that, dumb-skat," Yegor grunted. "We can't see a thing. How you gonna know who to hurt?"

"I dunno. That's future me problems. Lessbest case. . . Ima break everyone's neck."

"I'd like that," I mumbled numbly.

"Of course! Your sarding *Mal'svoloc*, Halfwit. *We* break bowls, less the other way around."

Flash. Bang. Scream.

Musket fire erupted from the mouths of the cavern in waves. The spray of rocks zapped my skin with the passage of lead-slicing air. The voices of chaos shuddered into a momentarily stunned silence and then into true fear. Not because of the thud of bodies falling lifeless to the ground, but because of the chorus of pain that filled the space. It was far easier to accept a silent death than it was to hear the agonies of those wracked in sufferance.

Someone fell onto me, taking me to the ground. The rattling breath was fleeting. Whoever it was had died. My leg felt damp and then wet. Another volley of musket fire peppered the cavern, I thought I might have been struck. Touching the wet spot, then my nose, I realized it was piss. Sour and rich. The scent proclaimed severe dehydration. Meekly, I pushed the corpse. It was heavy. It could only be a Big. I pushed again but harder this

WALKTALL

61

time. The body rolled away and I sat up, rising with the strike of far-off lamplight. As suddenly as it had come, the darkness abated.

Blinking I tried to make sense of it all. So many of us were dead or on the way. The *Mal'svoloc*, or what remained huddled beside me—Peter was hurt. Skat if I cared though. Skat if the Nils twins cared either. For beside me lay Hair Harold. Dead in a pool of his own blood and piss—the same piss that soaked my leg. Yegor and Marchovich rushed to my side, pushing me away, shaking Harold, desperately trying to wake him. It did not work. My gaze ran the length of Harold's corpse. Even in death, he was composed. Lengths of his golden hair splayed the ground like spun gold and the lamp light danced off the greasy starts of his beard. His eyes were glazed and although they no longer touted the twinkle of his confidence, they still held its shade with surprising alacrity. His mouth hung open, no doubt an echo of the pain afflicted, and yet all I could imagine was him calling me by my name—*Halfwit*.

The Bad Men leveled their muskets and prepared to fire at the few who remained. I squeezed my eyes shut. It was over and I knew it. Yet my death never came.

"Compeers," ruffled a muffled voice. Opening my eyes, I saw the man from before—Liverspots. He was as immaculate as always, dressed as if expecting a banquet of Trusted. Amid the stern-faced cadre of musket-wielding Bad Men, Liverspots wore a mask of weary kindness. He said something, softer this time, but too low for me to understand. I uncovered my ringing ears. *When had I covered them?*

" . . . rule was broken. It is a shame, for your class was nearly the first to pass the test of patience. Alas, some of you ran from this cave, and so you have been punished, thought it always makes me lesshappy to do so." Liverspots waved a hand, motioning to the wounded, dead, and dying—only a handful of us remained unscathed. "Compeers, the first rule was most easy to know, but the second part is not. Now that you have proven yourself lessobedient it would be a dereliction of my duty not to inquire further. Can one of you tell me, the only other rule I gifted to you?"

Silence.

"Come now? Must my men un more?"

This got us talking.

"To, to, to unname?"

"Yes, mostgood!" Liverspots praised. "What is your name, child?"

"Ein Mikell," the Little said, rising shakily to his feet. A musket fired. Collapsing, the boy stumbled and then crumpled into a pile, a look of shock frozen on his sallow face. Nodding, the guard set about reloading his firearm; smoke from his previous shot lacing its way into the cave, joining the cloud of musket-mist already within.

Liverspots pursed his lips and then continued as if nothing had happened.

"Shame. Now there is only eight of you children. But now you know the gift for lessobedience." Clasping his hands behind his back, he examined those that remained. "This rule may make lesssense to you today, but I say to you that there is power in a name. Tell me the true names of your compeers and you will feast and sleep in beds from here on." Greedy eyes scanned the room. It was plain to see who knew names and who did not. It was even plainer when they all began to shout.

"Gleb Peter!" shouted Yegor, leveling a finger at the stricken Little.

WALKTALL

Flash! Bang! Stagger!

"Yegor, why?" Peter grunted softly, clasping his belly, but doing little to staunch the growing red blemish.

"But he's a *Mal'svoloc!* We're family," Marchovich said, wide-eyed.

"Oh, grow up, Marco. *We're* family. We owe them nothing! You gonna really let this kid stand between us and getting out of here."

Who said we were getting out of here? I wondered.

Marchovich seemed to consider his brother's words.

"Marco," Peter paled. "Please."

But the twin shook his head. "Sorry Peter, but you ain't making it long anyways. We might as well get something out of it." Pointing Peter out, Yegor proclaimed the name for all to hear once more. One of the Bad Men approached to finish the job, killing him with a crack of the baton—like a fish to be clubbed.

Another voice piped up, another name was uttered, and another Big was slain.

"Anyone else?" Liverspots asked. Our eyes met. Gooseflesh prickled my skin. He smiled faintly. It scared me.

"You ain't saying nothin, Halfwit," Yegor growled at me. "Be a good idiot and keep that tongue of yours still."

I nodded, clasping Harold by the hand. I was a *Mal'svoloc.* Family didn't rat family, at least that's what I believed Harold would have done.

64

IZAIC YORKS

"Leave off him, Yegor. He ain't ever said anyone's name 'cept Harold's. I lessthink he even knows ours."

Yegor nodded, making sure to show me his fist—in case I needed any more convincing.

"That is it then?" Liverspots aksed, never breaking eye contact with me.

Silence.

"So, it is. In that case your reeducation begins tomorrow. Those of you who were mostcooperative will go with these men for your gifts. I hope you doubleplusmostenjoy them. The rest of you may come this way. . .

Filing out of the cavern, shaky, distraught, and ready for change, I was quick to move past Liverspots. Those stormy eyes of his pierced my soul, reading it, and then hanging it out to dry. I didn't know what was to come, but I did know one thing, and it was that Liverspots knew I wasn't a halfwit—even though I no longer knew it.

Rule, Second

. . .thus act as if your compeers are the living unned and neither see them, hear them, or speak to them, for they will hurt you. All hurt come from them and all gifts from us. Doublepluslessthings are yours and doubleplusall is the Lord Primes and the Future. . .do as mosttold and with mostdoublelessquestion. . .

-*Says Liverspots to the Children*

POD

Six became two pods of three.

Halfwit, they, and they.

Two boys and one girl.

Two Littles and one Big.

Three orphans—neither child nor adult.

Innocence stolen?

Who in the Deep said we were innocent?

Miss Anisha

First Class

Halfwit

"Stand straight! Side by side and lesssay a word until *she* allows it," barked the Bad Men. The large, fat-lipped man waved his fist to show us he meant business. Minutes earlier, me and my pod had been dragged from the confines of our cell and into this strange room. We were in a classroom with wooden floors, masoned walls, a blackboard, and old wooden desks. How they built it in the heart of the caves was beyond me. It almost made me feel like I was back in the city.

We, the children, were dressed in cream-colored uniforms, gifted by Liverspots. Yegor stood to one side—a thick simple eye patch now worn upon his face—and a girl on the other. She was missing a hand—well, mostly. No wonder she had been rounded up with us all. Street ladies generally required more than one working hand. She had a sweet face. One that made me wish we could be friends, but that couldn't happen. Liverspots had been plain as a day when it came to the second rule, and after the display in the cavern, I wasn't about to test him.

WALKTALL

"That will be all," spoke our would-be teacher. Her voice was shrill and cutting. I heard the click of her heels crossing the even, polished floor. I didn't dare look up. I could feel the girl next to me tremble, her shoulder shuddering against mine, and on the other side, Yegor stiffened.

The woman came to a stop in front of me. Her clogs were plain, oiled leather, with a small heart embellishing the right side. Her dress was long, only showing the white of her ankles. I did not dare to look higher for fear of being hurt.

I'm a halfwit! Nothing else.

"Compeer," the woman said, pausing and then repeating herself a moment later.

I'm a halfwit. Nothing else...

"Listen when the Lord Prime's Junto speaks," roared the Bad Man from before. He hit me across the head, the butt of his musket knocking me to my knees. My eyes watered and my head swam. My tummy spasmed, threatening to dump my previous meal across the woman's shoes and oiling them in an entirely different manner.

"I'm sorry," I screeched. Snot running down my nose.

"Then get up and doubleplusmostlisten! You can still be unned even though you made it this far—"

"*Enough!*" snapped the woman. "Now leave, before I have you also recommended for re-education."

"Yes, Miss Anisha," stuttered the man, the gusto suddenly absent from his voice. "As you say ma'am." He all but ran out of the classroom, the door closing with heavily behind him.

I cried, my head still clamoring with the alarm bells of pain. I touched where he had struck me. There was a fat welt.

"Dear, oh dear," Miss Anisha tutted. "This won't do." Kneeling down, the woman pulled me to my knees and then helped me to my feet. It wasn't a kind helping, but a rather brusque, pushy sort of help. "This is no place for tears," Miss Anisha said. "Wipe them away. Now."

Sniffling, I did as she said, looking properly at her at last. Not a hair was out of place on her head, hazel strands twined with slots of grey and pulled back into a sleek ponytail, so taught it might just peel the skin off her skull. Her skirt was black with a white collar, and her demeanor was like that of a bird. Just like me, her eyes were white as snow.

"There, that's better," she said looking at our sorry lot. "One iridan and two hasbish mongrels," she muttered under her breath. "It isn't likely any of you colored eyes will make it but I will try my best." Smoothing the folds of her dress she sniffed, her swiveling head coming to a rest. Her gaze was like that of an owl. It bore into us.

"Tell me, have you figured out why you are here? Anyone?"

The ticking of the clock filled some of the gap and our hissing breath the rest. Yegor answered brash and loud. "Because you are from the Deep and we are being tested!"

WALKTALL

71

"In a manner," Miss Anisha said, "But we are hardly from the Deep. Religion is tlessreal. I am of flesh and blood. Anyone else?" She looked at me again, this time expectantly.

I am a halfwit. Nothing more, I thought, biting my tongue.

Finally, the girl beside me spoke, timid and innocent. "You are culling us."

"Certainly." Miss Anisha almost smiled. A flicker, a twitch of the lip. "How do you know that?"

"I had an uncle who was assigned to the slaughterhouses," the girl said.

"You are a bright one," Miss Anisha nodded. "Let us wish, for your sake, that I can *squash* that." A cold sweat ran down my back at the way she said it—the delight she took in the prospect of grinding us down.

"You are the remaining few, the ones who have proven your ability to follow the rules. The malleable few who are to be forged into the next Lord Prime. By the end of our time, only one of you shall remain. You won't be more than a vessel of our master's will. If the prospect of that is too much to bear, then speak now and you will be unned."

We were silent. I wondered if the others also held their tongues on account of cowardice. I certainly did.

"So be it," Miss Anisha said, "then we will begin with names. From now on you are First Student and you Second and you Third. . ."

REEDUCATION

Twelfth Class

Halfwi - S

I knew better than to glance about, but Miss Anisha wasn't there yet. She wouldn't be for a few more minutes, because that is how things were. We arrived early, standing at attention with our hands flat against our sides, and she arrived on time. The clock clicked. Louder than a pigeon cooing over lost bread. I stared ahead.

Tick, tick, tick, pestered the clock. A plain thing set on Miss Anisha's plain desk—always ordered neatly with plain pens and plain ink. I glanced back and forth.

"Student two," crowed Miss Anisha, shutting the door behind her. Your eyes are wandering."

I snapped my gaze forward, too afraid to trace her steps to the center of the room and before us. As usual, she looked neither pleased nor dissatisfied.

Miss Anisha just was.

"Good day, compeers," she said. Whether it was day or not, I cared not—reality existed as I was told. At her greeting we saluted, touching our knuckles

WALKTALL

73

to our mouth, and pressing the opposite hand—or part hand in Student Three's case—into the base of our back.

"Good day, Miss Anisha!" we thundered, trying our best to toe the line between overly enthusiastic and authentic; in our first few classes, she had made us practice just greetings until I thought my brain might burst.

She nodded and then signed the greeting to us again, this time wiggling her fingers and motioning with her arms.

Good day, Miss Anisha, we said, using the sign language she had taught us thus far.

She nodded. I felt a small thrill of exhilaration. She was happy with our delivery. If we got everything else right, then we would get sweet bread with supper.

"Recite the anthem."

"Land of light and peace behold.

bless the Almighty's heart. . ."

So, we sang. When we were finished, she implored us to recite the Lord Prime's creed. It was boring, and numbing, and I didn't believe it for the least, but if I wanted to eat it was what I had to do. Once we had finished civics, Miss Anisha extolled us with the goodness of the Lord Primes rule. The promise of utopia and the role we must all play to see it come to fruition. Repeating after her, we condemned the sins of our forefathers and condemned the living sin with which their actions implicated upon us. For my part, she encouraged me to hate them on account of their eyes and to see the wrongdoing of their ancestors first. Personally, I didn't understand the first thing of what she was saying and so—just like everything else—I went through the motions.

Soon it was time for our daily test.

"Student Three," Miss Anisha said, "how would you atone for the crime of your forbearers?"

"If asked to, I would whip myself clean of the sin, though it would lesserase it," said the girl.

"And how far must you be willing to go to atone?"

"Unto un."

Miss Anisha nodded and turned to address me.

"Student Two, you have just learned that Student Three is the beneficiary of iridan slavery, what do you do?"

"I would alert the authorities and lead them to her."

"As the first claimer, what is your right if Student Three is proven lessinnocent?"

"As an iridan or hasbian?" I could feel Yegor seething beside me. He didn't much like being duped into thinking I was little more than a halfwit. What could I say? I was a good teaser.

"Which are you?" Miss Anisha admonished—more than a little annoyed at my asking. A ding on my part. I winced.

"Iridan, Miss Anisha."

"Then show me."

WALKTALL

75

"I would be gifted one stoning for each generation of iridan slavery supported by her ancestors and a fifth of her property."

Miss Anisha clapped her hands and I jumped. *Did I say something wrong?*

"You were to *show* me. Disobedience has only remedy, I am afraid. Squat, all of you, and hands straight. I want to see your palms," Miss Anisha said. Mechanically, the three of us moved into the position and awaited her instructions. Beside me, Yegor growled low enough so that only I could hear. If he could flay me open, fish out my liver, and use it to catch a shark, I think he would have.

"Sing the anthem and continue until I say otherwise. One note out of place and the longer we practice in this position."

"Land of light and peace behold

bless the Almighty's heart. . . "

So we sang over and over and over until Yegor's voice cracked, and then we sang again and again and again until I missed a word, the lines blurring together into one slush muddle of lyrics, and then we sang more and more and more until our limbs burned, our knees screamed, our backs creaked, our arms drooped, and *then* we sang over and again and more until Student Three collapsed in a quivering pitiful pile. *Then* the badmen came in at the crow of Miss Anisha's voice, to strap us with leather until our backs pruned with cherry welts.

That was when the singing finally came to an end.

"You are all very doublepluslessgood children today. You lesscare for the future or goodness of our Lord Prime. Tonight, none of you shall eat until you can show your loyalty in all things. Additionally, for Student Two's disobedience at the beginning of today's lesson, both Student One and Three shall have their blankets confiscated for the eve.

Straightening her spectacles and clasping pale hands behind her back, Miss Anisha left the classroom, as the Bad Men escorted us to our cells.

COMPELLED

Twelfth Class

Halfwi - S

He clobbered me across the brow, burying my vision in a screen of sticky red, prying the blanket from my grasp. Wiping the blood from my eyes, I growled in defiance. I was small for my age but nowhere close to being a full-time coward. "That's mine," I screeched, launching myself at Yegor, and snatching at the ragged edges.

"It's your fault they took ours! I deserve this!" Yegor snarled, favoring his good eye. Balling his fingers into a fist he struck me in the gut, driving the air from my lungs. "Pathetic, weak halfwit," he snorted, ambling to his corner of our pod's tiny cell. Settling onto his pallet—wood with a mattress stuffed with wool—he scowled at me and said, "I dun' see what Hair Harold saw in you."

My belly turned like the churning of the waves, but somehow I managed to keep my stomach and all its contents.

"You have no right to say his name," I fumed.

78 IZAIC YORKS

"He had lessright to tell it," Yegor growled. "If I knew yours, I'd tell Liverspots just for the chance at some lamb stew."

"But we were the *Mal'svoloc,*" I said. "We were a family!"

"You are such a Little," Yegor growled darkly. "Grow up why dun' you? I was a sarding *Potercha* before this and before that, I had an *actual* family! The kind with a mother and father. We are what we have to be, but you know all about that dun' you *Halfwit?*"

"You were a *Potercha*?" Third Student squeaked, at the mention of the most notorious street gang in all of Hasbal. "But they—"

"What? Killed Littles, dogs, and whatever else we could sacrifice to the Deep Ones? The only way to keep bad luck away is to make deals with the Deep. Everyone knows the Almighty is too high up to see *our* kind."

The logical part of my brain wanted to shout, to ask what good that had done for him, but instead my body crashed into his.

We rolled across the floor, spilling the latrine bucket all over the blanket and our clothes. That really pissed Yegor off.

"Imma un you!"

"Try it and see what happens you bastard. You heard Miss Anisha, only one of us will make it anyways, I might as well make my chances better!"

Third Student cried, begging us to stop, but we didn't care. I bit Yegor in the shoulder, breaking the skin. He hammered me twice on the head, knocking me free. Before I could respond he was on my back, one arm around my windpipe and the other pulling entire tufts of my hair free. "End of the road," Yegor huffed, pushing my face into the rocky floor.

WALKTALL

79

Pebbles, dirt, and more filled my vision, nostril, ear, and mouth, but what I desperately needed I could not find—*air*. Bucking, I tried to throw him free, but I only succeeded in transitioning us, so that we lay on my side. The cell seemed to flip as my orientation and disorientation collided into one. Far and away, as if standing at the end of a tunnel, Third Student took center stage of my sight. Her mouth was moving, tears streaking her face.

At first, I thought she was praying. But there was no mistaking the soprano notes in her voice. She was singing.

"Land of light and peace behold

bless the Almighty's heart..."

My mouth parted unable to vocalize the words but moving in concert with hers. It was the strangest sensation, like an itch that had to be appeased. Even stranger, the brassy tenor of Yegor's voice joined lockstep with hers and his arms slackened. Not one to be told twice, I wrestled myself free and crawled away as fast as I could, and collapsing in a coughing fit upon my own pallet. Confusion crossed Yegor's face as he stared at his own hands and he too fled to his bed. And even though I was still raw from the crush of Yegor's grip, I sang.

"For duty, for sacrifice, come compeer

the perfect future is ours."

None of us dared move when the song came to an end. None of us understood what had happened. But I believed that if not for Third Student, I would not be alive. Reeking of bile and shit, I poked my hand into a sliver in my mattress and fished around until I found what it was I sought.

80

IZAIC YORKS

Retrieving a biscuit that I had squirreled away from the prior night's supper, I shakily found my feet and hesitantly approached Third Student.

"I lessmeant it. I lessmeant to interrupt," she said scurrying away from me, despite being a good inch taller.

Raising my hands, I showed her the biscuit. Cautious at first, she took my offering, her eyes glancing to the gate of our cell. As usual, the room was empty, save for the flicker of the lamp and the droning of the clock, with a ticking so loud it often woke us from our sleep. Biting into the stale food, her eyes lit up. Sighing, she gave thanks to the Almighty and the Lord Prime. Then she devoured it. Moments later only crumbs remained of the buttery treat.

Licking the remains from her fingers, one by one, leaving a residue of swirled flour and saliva behind, she finally asked, "Why?"

"Just a thank you," I whispered hoarsely, retreating back to my pallet. Glancing back at Yegor, I saw him rocking back and forth, still staring at his hands; and even though I knew the Big wouldn't be giving me any more trouble this day, I still hardly slept a wink. Privately, I wondered if the Lord Prime actually could hear our prayers. I didn't want to believe it, but if Miss Anisha said it, then so it was.

If Miss Anisha says it, so it is, so it is, so itis... then I prayed as I had been taught.

SPACES BETWEEN

"I miss skyr over twisted dough, summertide mornings, and playing chase under the bridges."

"Well, I miss the smell of rain on cobblestone and the feel of Czester's by the fireplace."

"Czester? Do you have boyfriend or something?"

"What! No! It's the bitch at Madam Else's. I always tried to pet her while listening to the Strollers tell their stories."

"The old domino one?"

"Yes! Wait. . . have you been to Madam Else's?"

"Uh, once. I found a spot to listen and sleep last Pax Nomus."

"Doublepluslessway! I was there too! Do you remember the story?"

"Who would lessso? It was so good! I mostlike stories about the Ascendants."

"Yea, me doubleplustoo. Oh, how I wish I was an Ascendant, or if I even knew one."

"Fat chance of that," Third Student whispered with a yawn. "I'm going to sleep."

"Yea, me too," I said, closing my eyes and drifting off to sweet dreams. They were filled with the smell of birch floors, stewing meats, drooling hounds, and the gentle bask of Madam Else's hearth.

I was happy.

Like Clay

Thirty-Fourth Class

Hal - Secon

Sweat slipped along the slope of my armpit and dribbled slowly along the small of my back, bidden by what Miss Anisha called our "daily calisthenics."

"Lessthings cleanse the soul like physical work. March! Double time!"

We picked up the pace, not too fast not too slow, for only Miss Anisha knew how long we would be doing this. Though the "room" was only a handful of strides long we marched. Back and forth. Forth and back. Turning, with a drilled military precision, just before our noses touched the walls. It was numbing and not to mention exhausting. Some days we drilled from breakfast to supper—assuming we got either of those meals.

Keeping my eyes straight, I hardly noticed the starry twinkle of the cavern walls. They glinted in the lamplight, heavenly pinpricks breaking a midnight cloud, ranging in color from plum to silver to gold. I heard First Student and Third Student raising their voices and so I followed suit; eager not to seem uninterested, and actually half believing that I was excited to be taking part in the day's exercise.

"I denounce my crimes! I denounce the crimes of our fathers! I denounce the lessgood of the hasbish! I thank the Lord Prime, my savior by the power of the Almighty! My life belongs to our future! To live for utopia is to *un* while being *un-unned*! I denounce my crimes. . ."

At first, I had thought this repetition strange. I was an orphan, a member of a street gang, just another kid. I cared little for this great and golden future, but as each day blurred into the next, the monotony of it all shattered my resolve, one chip at a time, until I actually believed it.

"I denounce my crimes! I denounce the crimes of our fathers! I denounce the lessgood of the hasbish! I thank the Lord Prime, my savior by the power of the Almighty! My life belongs to our future! To live for utopia is to un while being un-unned! I denounce my crimes. . ."

I marched back and forth. Forth and back.

"I denounce my crimes! I denounce the crimes of our fathers! I denounce the lessgood of the hasbish! I thank the Lord Prime, my savior by the power of the Almighty! My life belongs to our future! To live for utopia is to un while being un-unned! I denounce my crimes. . ."

I marched back and forth. Forth and back. I didn't need to look about to see if I was in time with Third Student and First Student, I mean Yegor, *no, First Student.*

"I denounce my crimes! I denounce the crimes of our fathers! I denounce the lessgood of the hasbish! I thank the Lord Prime, my savior by the power of the Almighty! My life belongs to our future! To live for utopia is to un while being un-unned! I denounce my crimes. . ."

WALKTALL

85

I marched back and forth. Forth and back. I didn't need to look about to see if I was in time with Third Student and First Student, I mean Yegor, *no, First Student.*

My eyes glazed over, almost in a trance. I hardly noticed the spooling of natural light that fed into the cavern from above, until a shadow, brief as it was, broke the only sunlight available in this deep place. My eyes flicked up and my head followed, craning to seek the disruption of the chimney's light. I expected to see a bat flitting about, awakened by the annoyance of our presence, but the obstruction was not of the flying variety. Peering out of the rocky hole was a girl's face, curious and familiar. An ode from a past that was so close and yet felt little more than a distant dream.

"Rutoff," I gasped, the words feeling foreign in my mouth.

Shaking her head, she pushed a finger to her mouth and vanished beyond the chimney's lip.

I blinked, faltering out of step, and losing the conviction of my words. Pinching myself I checked to see that I wasn't asleep. No, what I had seen was real. My mind whirled towards the fantastic and I feared that I had seen a ghost.

"Second Student," Miss Anisha said, with a tone like claws scraping a chalkboard. "What are you doing?"

"I'm sorry," I blubbered incoherently, returning to the realm of reality.

"Your city, your Lord Prime, and the future are doublelesslooking for excuses. Why should you be lessput in the hole?"

The blood drained from my face and my knees went weak. *Anything but there.* It had only taken one experience in that solitary place to learn that I never wanted to go back. Memories of that suffocating, breath-stealing, dreaded darkness consumed me.

"Teacher, I messed up! I forgot where I was. It is my honor to be here, my mostgift that I am of the chosen! I would give everything to the future." Snot and tears mixed into a salty, green alchemical brew.

I dared not look up.

Miss Anisha tutted softly to herself, the heel of her clogs clicking in time with the *ticking crack* of the clock. Seconds stretched to minutes. "I will believe you *if* you defer punishment to Third Student on account of the sins of her forefathers. Third Student moaned softly and judging from the sound of it, fell to her knees. Raising my head I could feel the relief warming my body with a jubilant tingle.

I could be free. She is a sinner after all. Just look at her, look at her eyes. But when I did all I saw was another orphan like myself—lost and alone. *But I can't go back, not there. She would do it to me if our roles were reversed, right? And what about that hand?* Likely mutilated for the offense of theft. *She is stupid and is a colored-eyed.* If there was any doubt in my mind that she should go to the hole instead of myself, it was erased.

So why couldn't I say it?

"Student Two," Miss Anisha said. "Choose now, otherwise I'll take your silence as acceptance of punishment."

My mouth moved but no sound came out.

WALKTALL

87

"Speak up and articulate as you have been taught."

Student Three looked at me pleadingly. I wanted desperately to say yes, but all I could manage was the caving of my shoulders, the bowing of my head, and a sob from my soul.

I couldn't do it. I wouldn't do it.

When the Bad Men came to collect me, I did not resist but allowed them to lift me away. As I passed Third Student our eyes met, and though words were not uttered, the essence of meaning managed to pass between the space of things.

Thank you.

HOLE

Darkness Never Ending

H - Second St

I was not happy. I was six feet underground. In a hole meant for a coffin. I hate small spaces.

Saucer-sized butterflies raced in my belly. My tongue was as dry as baked sand beneath the summertide sun. I tasted bile and smelled the musty dank begotten from wet soil. I struggled to breathe as if my chest had been bound with a belt. My feet ached from the hours spent standing—neither able to sit or lay. Wriggling my body, I tried to stretch the pain away but only succeeded in brushing up against the walls of the hole—only a finger-width away.

"Breathe. Breathe. Breathe."

Closing my eyes, I pretended that I was riding a great butterfly far and away from this place. I imagined cutting the emerald waves of the aurora upon a beast with great crystal wings—one so big a handful of children could join me. I tried to recall the icy jab of a cold night and what it felt like for it to pierce my hair and prickle my skin. But I couldn't remember.

WALKTALL

My heart raced, daring to beat right out of my chest.

"I lessremember," I sobbed, slamming my head on the walls of the hole until it throbbed in time with my heart.

I wasn't upset that I couldn't remember the things of my past. I was upset because I could no longer remember my name.

Something unseen scurried about my feet. A rat. They sometimes got in there. Its mangy side touched the skin of my leg and I tried to use my powers. I tried to rebuke it and send it on its way, but sometimes my magic didn't work, and this was one of those times. Its claws bit into my skin and it crawled up my side, squeaking all the way. "*Ahhhhhhhhhhhhhhhhhhhgh!*" I shrieked. Desperately, I clawed at the walls, vainly trying to flee this nightmare. Jagged nails, set just so, tore at my flesh, denying my feeble attempts at escape.

"Let me out!" I screamed, ignoring the throb in my hands. I yelled over and over, until my voice was hoarse, and my lips foamed with spittle, yet the casting above was never removed. Slivers of filtered light pricked through the holes of the cover, reaching teasingly down into my deep abode. I was alone. Dreadfully and terribly alone.

Falling into misery, I nearly missed his approach, the owner's boots clicking on the stone floors above.

"Please, please, please!" I begged as a shadow blotted out the light above. "I have doubleplusmostlearned. I mostwant to show my duty and sacrifice to the future. Believe me! I'm sorry!"

"What is your name?" The voice was as soft as honey and sweet as fruit on the cusp of decay. I knew him. He was the one who brought gifts when we were good. He was the one who cared. The one whose praise meant a night with a full belly and warm blanket in which to snuggle.

Liverspots breathed, the noise rattling in the space between our words.

"I don't know anymore," I answered truthfully, neither quickly nor slowly, but with the conviction of one who had nothing to hide.

There was a pause and then he said, "You will make Hasbal mostproud, I think. It pains me to know you are in here, but take heart, pearls are lessformed without pain. The strong always find a way."

He left and so the light returned. Stars in a deep, deep place. Again, I was alone. Dreadfully and terribly alone, and yet strangely proud.

BLUR

Thirty-Ninth Class? Twenty-Second Class? Sixty-fifth Class?

Second Student

Clinkety-clank goes the rattle of the keys, mornings come, evenings come, or perhaps the other way around, Bad Men escort us down halls of stone, some cavern, others marked by men, the days draw on, same-same, *tsk-tsk* says Miss Anisha running us through the drills, words flow from our mouths, promises of service and sacrifice, praise to our great city, hate for our past, over and over we repeat whether marching with word or giving a speech, little by little I forget, not just my name but all that I believe, there is only sacrifice, duty, and what they say, get it wrong and face the deep, get it right and Liverspots delights, round and round we go, *tick-tock* tolls the clock, sleeping or awake, eating or shitting, it makes no difference, for I live in a blur repeating the same again and over, spun by the potter's wheel and shaped by the master hand.

Vessel, I am.

GRETA

Second Student

"Do you think it will ever end," Third Student whispered from her pallet. As usual, we waited to talk until First Student was snoring away and the Bad Men had left us alone. Pulling my blanket under my chin, I curled into a ball and rolled to face her.

"Liverspots said we graduate tomorrow," I said. "After that we're free."

"Then what?" she asked, her face obscured by the shadows draping our cell. "Where do we go from here?"

I shrugged.

"Maybe this is what it takes to be Trusted?"

"You think?" she asked, propping herself up with her good hand. "That would be a gift," she added dreamily.

"That's what Miss Anisha says. What else could it be? You have to be Trusted before becoming Lord Prime. Think about it."

"I lessdo *that* anymore."

WALKTALL

93

"Yeah, me too," I agreed. We both knew that *thinking* hurt us more than it ever helped.

"Do you think we will know each other still?"

I shrugged. We both knew only one of us could be Lord Prime. We both hoped we might survive. We both didn't want to think about the odds of that.

"I doublepluslesscan forget you," she said. "You went to the hole for me. I am Hasbish, I *deserve* to be punished.

"You do," I agreed. Like second nature, the words flowed from me, even though I was not so sure I believed them. She seemed to wilt—just a little.

"But I like you," I quickly added. Then blushing, "You're the first girl I lessmind."

At that, she seemed to perk up. Even smile a little.

"You're halfgood, for a *boy*," she said, crawling from her pallet and into mine.

"What are you doing," I hissed, trying to push her away. Laying as far away from her as I could, without leaving the warm embrace of my little blanket, I tried to tell her to leave. She shook her head and waggled her tongue.

"I just wanted to say thank you for being my compeer," she whispered. Her words were light and airy, and her breath tickled my ears, reminding me of Madam Else's where we orphans would pack the room like sardines in a jar. Turning bright red, it dawned on me that *this* was a *girl*, and she was in *my* bed! Despite being an orphan and a Little, everyone knew what happened in beds between boys and girls. Well, at least the general idea. I wasn't too sure about the specifics.

"You're as red as the dawning banner at the springtide fest," she giggled.

"I. . . um, well I don't really know how this works," I admitted, feeling the wave of crimson expand down my back.

"What?" she breathed sharply. "I told you; I am doubleless a street lady."

Turning away from me she *harumphed* and called me something like an idiot. Embarrassment turned into sparks of anger and I pursed my lips. "How was I supposed to know? When boys and girls get in the same bed, they, you know. . ."

She sighed with exasperation.

"I'm lessapologizing," I whispered.

"Fine, then I will lesstalk."

"Fine. Get out of my bed."

"I will when you apologize."

I wanted to pull the hair from my head and yell at her, but that would have awoken First Student, and he didn't like that—so I seethed silently in annoyance.

"Girls are stupid and weird."

"Boys have heads thick as an ox."

Girls have cooties and make people sick."

WALKTALL

95

"Boys carry plagues and trip over their own feet. . ."

"Girls like silly things and that makes them silly just cause," I growled.

Rolling over she furrowed her brow and tried to pinch me, catching only air.

"There! I made you move," I said triumphantly, eliciting a murmur from Student One.

We both froze.

"Hush," she whispered, pushing a finger to my lips. For the second time, I froze. I had never been touched by a girl before—not counting my mother. Her hand was frosty to the touch and as calloused as chiseled rock, but to be touched by another human, one who truly cared for me, that was all I could ever ask for.

"Fine. You win. I forgive you."

"When did I apologize?"

"I am a lady," she said. "I can forgive whenever I want." I wanted to point out that actually, she was a girl, but I decided against it. "What's your name?"

"My name?" I blinked. "Like the real one?"

"Yes."

Thrice I blinked. I couldn't remember. I felt humiliated. Wracking my mind, I tried to pull it from the imprint of propaganda stamped over my memories, and though it dangled on the tip of my tongue, I could not recall.

I shook my head.

"I understand," she nodded. "The rules."

I nodded.

I was too much of a coward to admit otherwise.

"That's alright. Let me tell you mine."

"But the rules," I gagged, "if they find out you could be put in the hole or *worse*."

Peering past me and at the sleeping mass that was First Student, she shook her head, "You will protect my secret. I trust you."

If only she knew how close I had been to sending her to the hole. Shame seeped throughout my soul.

"Do not be afraid," she said. "My name is Iya Greta."

Taking my hand, she laced her fingers within mine, and for quite some time we shared in the moment of friendship, as only compeers might. I was happy.

LESSON LEARNED

Graduation

Second Student

Sitting at the head of the proctor table, Liverspots unlaced his fingers and peered down from his seat on high. Miss Anisha flanked his right and on his left sat a man I did not recognize. The Junto examined me. Their robes were gilded red and bronze with buttons of brass and sashes of white. The tall hats they wore were every bit as rich as the room. Art framed in gold dressed the walls, polished wood reflected the light, and a wall of books guarded the rear. Saluting, the Bad Men left the room, leaving me alone with my scrutinizers. Silently, I stood at attention, awaiting my first order.

Thankfully, it wasn't long in coming.

"Second Student," Liverspots said, his stormy gaze grazing mine. "You are the last and final student to stand the test before this Junto. How do you present?"

"With all that my soul has to offer," I said mechanically—just as Miss Anisha had drilled me.

"If it is wanting, so shall it soon be determined."

I quietly gulped. I wasn't certain what he meant. Orphans swiftly learned to read tones if they wanted to survive, and Liverspots's voice implied: *or else.*

"We shall begin with a singing of the anthem."

Clearing my throat...

"Land of light and peace behold

bless the Almighty's heart...

...For duty, for sacrifice, come compeer

the perfect future is ours."

I finished with a practiced note, one that dipped as low as I could muster without breaking pitch. Then I fell to one knee, gave thanks with a salute, and rose back to attention. If they were pleased *or* upset, the Junto did not show it. Instead, they droned on as if nothing had occurred.

"This board shall ask you a series of questions. Answer to the best of your ability."

I stared ahead. Straight ahead. I dared not do anything else.

Adjusting his monocle, the man to the left wheezed out his question with a voice that sounded like it had been scorched by dragon fire. "To whom do we owe the modern era?"

"To Von Lucas," I said without hesitation. "He exposed the plots of Sash, the Lord Ascendant, and ended the cycle of slavery." Ash-Breath nodded, pushing the spectacles up the bridge of his nose. Miss Anisha was next. "For what ends has the Lord Prime frozen the innovation?"

WALKTALL

99

Another easy one.

"Technology and power deceive us into thinking we're more than we are. It makes materialists of us and soulless compeers," I said, signing what I spoke with near perfection.

Miss Anisha gave a slight nod of the head. I was doing well. Really well.

"What are the three signs that shall herald utopia?" Liverspots asked softly.

I nearly smiled it was all too easy. *Tonight, I'm gonna eat like the Lord Prime,* I was certain of it.

"Evil shall disappear from man. All needs will be met and all will be as one family."

Liverspots smiled, warming me with pride. Looking at both his counterparts he all but purred, "This one is ready for our final question and test."

Test? I thought, fighting to keep my face placid. *Isn't this all a test? What could he mean?*

"Your final question," Liverspots said, "is as follows, what *are* you?"

I sighed—it wasn't a hard one.

"I am a sacrifice of duty for the perfect future."

"And your previous identities?"

"I am an *un-unned* what came before I no longer know."

And it was true, and they knew it.

Clapping his hands, I nearly jumped at the sudden *crack*, Liverspots rose to a stand—the others following his example. The door to the room opened, and to my horror, the Bad Men drug her in. Two of them, one for each arm, throwing her between me and the high table. My compeer curled into a ball—weeping, battered, and bruised.

Greta.

I wanted to run to her and tell her it would be alright. But it was obvious, wasn't it? She must have failed her test, otherwise, they wouldn't have done this to her. Betraying the parts of me that were still good and great, I watched as she wept into her hand.

"This one broke the first rule and must be punished. She will be unned either way, but whether it swift or not is entirely up to you." At Liverspots words the Bad Men affixed their kiats, short knifing bayonets, to the ends of their muskets. Greta didn't look up this time but instead sobbed harder at the declaration. My pulse quickened, my chest tightened, and my vision swam. Memories of the hole came to the fore, making matters worse. My breath hastened and the only thing that kept me from passing out was the sight of my one, and only compeer.

We were supposed to graduate, to escape, to become Trusted! The edges of my eyes grew damp and the sounds of the world dulled beneath the beating of my heart.

"Second Student. Second Student. What will it be?" Liverspot called. He might as well have been a blot in the distance.

"You see?" Miss Anisha said. "I told you he is too soft."

"Na," Liverspots said. "He has all the tools, he has taken the imprinting well, the magic will do the rest."

"Call him again," Ash-Breath implored.

"You have until I count to five, Second Student."

My breath quickened and yet I was never able to get enough.

"One," Liverspots said.

I won't. I can't turn Greta in.

"Two. . ."

I remembered the feeling of her hand in mine, cool and comforting.

"Three. . ."

I looked at Bad Men preparing to skewer her over and over with their wicked kiats.

If I run between them then maybe we can both be unned. Together.

"Four. . ."

Sniffling, Greta pushed herself up to her knees. Though she was still crying, she began to sing, and I began to sing. Our eyes met and so flowed the words in the spaces between things.

Greta nodded, giving me permission, a look of understanding in her eyes. As if she knew what I had to do, and wanted to let me know she had already forgiven me. My lips felt locked, my tongue heavy—what I would have done then to tear it from my mouth.

"Five."

"Iya Greta, that is her name." I declared.

Liverspots blinked, a look of satisfaction crossing his face.

"Well done, well done. The strong always find a way." Nodding to the Bad Men he gave them permission to end her life, which they did—effecient and quick.

If Greta suffered, it wasn't long. Watching the light fade from her eyes, I didn't resist the Bad Men who came to collect me, nor did I acknowledge what Liverspots had to say. Something about the final pieces of my transformation—*skat* if I cared. My compeer was gone and by my word. Pulled from the room I could not understand why in her last moments she sang:

"Thank you."

Rule, Third

. . .Your voice is our voice. Our voice is utopia's voice. Doubleknow and abide your doubleplustmostless voice. . .

-Says Liverspots to Second Student

SOUNDS

First, there is the sounds of the straps being fastened, then tightened.

Kachink. Schwick.

Then the sound of my body protesting and fighting as my feet kick about.

Tha-thump! Tha-thump!

Followed by the crack of a baton to knock me out.

Whapam!

After this, the physician admonishes the Bad Men for being so rough.

"The lad is due for surgery, idiots. I less want to deal with triage and treatment of a concussion.

Then comes the good stuff. Like the sound of the first scalpel being pulled from the flames.

Shhick.

Followed by fingers prying my drooling, lolling mouth apart.

"Blaaaaaaah schtaaaaap. . ."

Which is only answered by the sawing of my tongue from my mouth.

Chaschik shachikkkkshshshshsh chikleghhhhk

My screams, the only thing free as multiple hands hold me down.

"MAAAAAAAAAAAAAAAAAAAAAAAA..."

Then comes the second scalpel from the flames as my tongue comes free.

Shhick.

Pressed into my mouth, burning the sides and cauterizing the wound.

Shhhhhhhhhhhhhhhhhhhhhh

The beat of my heart, out of control.

Babumpbabumpbabumpbabump

And at last the sweet hold of darkness as my consciousness fades.

That has no sound.

FEVER DREAM

Second Student

Second Student

Thank you. I dreamed of Greta's death nonstop. The world of my sleep no longer provided escape but now replayed the horrors of my reality. In one nightmare, Liverspots began his counting once more, and the anxiety in my chest was like a bull trying to burst free. I fevered through one horror after the next. Soup bowls, always empty. Singing under Miss Anisha's yoke until my throat bled raw. And now. . . something in this dream was different.

There was another presence.

All else faded away until it was just they and I.

We stood in that room, richly adorned before, but now empty of the Junto, the Bad Men, and poor Greta.

"Who's there?" I asked, shielding my eyes from the bright light that seemed to emanate from all about their presence. Slowly that figure approached, from where I could not say, their silhouette taking on further detail as their aura began to fade.

"Harold," I breathed. I clamped my hands to my mouth, afraid that I had just betrayed him too.

"Ja, ja, ja," Harold chuckled, full of health and color as I had never known him. "You worry too much Halfwit, its only a dream."

"Halfwit?" I asked, vaguely remembering the name. Harold frowned a look of sadness breaking his usual, jolly self.

"Ja. That is the name I gave you."

"I remember," I said, recalling the times before. "It kept trouble away. Everyone was too scared to mess with me."

"Well, I always did know how to recognize a good teaser. Did you ever learn anything about Liverspots?"

I didn't ask how he knew my nickname for the man.

"Na," I said, shuffling my feet.

"Never mind that," Harold said. "It seems nothing went to plan."

I looked him hard in the face and furrowed my brow.

"Was there ever really a plan?"

"Ja, ja! To survive of course! Which *you* are doing a fine job of," he said, slapping me on the back.

"Harold, I unned someone to do it though."

Waving his hands, he laughed me off. "I would be shocked if you hadn't." Crossing his arms, his face became stony and his temperament grave.

WALKTALL 109

"Halfwit, you have to listen to me."

"What else am I supposed to do?" I asked sarcastically. "We're in a dream. At least I am anyways. . ."

"Ja, ja, ja. Seriously."

I raised my hands. It wasn't like there was much else to do.

"The Bad Men have gone, Halfwit. You are sleeping on a bed in the physician's room. The door is unlocked. You must wake up and follow Peter. This is your only chance to escape."

I would have laughed if not for the expression on his face.

"Do you realize how stupid that sounds?"

"Do you realize how weird this dream is," Harold retorted.

I nodded but I wasn't convinced. Opening my mouth to respond, Harold sighed, "Here I thought it was only a nickname." He kicked me in the crotch, and I cursed his name right unto waking.

SARDING DEEP!

The blankets, damp with sweat fell off of me as I jerked awake, the words in my mind never actually leaving my mouth. Pain, unlike anything I had ever known, erupted through my mouth, expanding into trickling tingles all along my skull. I nearly passed out, but miraculously I somehow managed not to. Calming myself, I found that I was in a bed, unrestrained, in a room brimming with physician supplies, with a door left ever so slightly ajar.

Whimpering I felt my lips. I stifled a cry. Then I wailed a short, horrible, wet, and gurgling noise. Despite the absence of my tongue, it felt as if my mouth had been stuffed full. My eyes watered just thinking about it.

Blinking, I found my feet and tiptoed hesitantly to the door. Carefully pulling it open I peered out.

Nothing. Nobody was there and the tunnels surely wound into the maze that was this deep, evil place. I had been so busy with surviving that I hadn't ever the time to even begin unwinding the mess that was Vysegors. Two thoughts raced into my mind at once; run for my life, maybe escape, or likely become lost, get caught, and killed.

I knew what I *wasn't* going to do. I *wasn't* going to run out there! I had come this far to die from stupidity.

I'm not a halfwit.

I trembled, struck by the word, by the name, by a part of who I had been.

Halfwit. Halfwit. Halfwit!

I shook with excitement, forgetting the red-hot fever that savaged my body.

I wanted to shout it to the world, but I didn't dare try, for fear of the pain.

Instead, I jumped up and down, reclaiming the small sliver of who I had been.

That's when I saw it. Another Little stared at me, not far from the door.

Peter. But how?

WALKTALL

The sandy-haired boy seemed to hear my thoughts and bowed. Straightening, he mouthed for me to follow. I blinked and rubbed my eyes and pinched my skin.

It can't be true.

Yet it was.

I glanced back at the bed, where I should be, and then once more at the boy in the tunnel. I made the choice only a halfwit would. I took chase after my compeer. But before I did, I paused to ruffle through the physician's things. Finding what I sought, I followed after Peter—the silver scalpel glinting in my clenched fist.

Peter ran, always just ahead of me, turning this way and that—unfazed by the countless junctions and intersections. I sprinted as fast as my legs could carry me, and every time that I thought I might lose him the Little slowed, just enough for me to keep apace. I passed wooden doors, gilded caverns, squalid places, and halls of rubble. Where we were going I had no idea.

Just as the heat of my breath scorched the nub of my tongue, and the fever seemed at its worst, we finally arrived. Peter had led me to a dead end. An alcove of rock and other debris. Waving the scalpel, I wanted to scream, but again he smiled his impish grin and disappeared into the wall. No, he crawled into a hole, dark and small.

Shaking my head, I staggered away. I couldn't go in there. Not such a small space. I would rather die. Sinking to my knees I punched the ground at Peter's betrayal. *How could he take me to what I feared most?* Memories of the hole swamped me, suffocating and crushing. Whimpering, I began to cry.

"*Compeer?*"A familiar voice sounded.

Greta? I wondered looking about wild-eyed.

"Have valor, compeer. If you stay here you will be unned."

I would take that a hundred times over going in there!

"Then it would all be in vain. You must survive, compeer."

But you were unned. If I am too then at least I could join you and all my compeers.

"Sweet compeer. I let myself be unned so that you could survive. Would you make light of my sacrifice?"

I had no words with which to refute, no rationale, only guilt.

"It is your duty to survive".

I can't breathe in there, I thought, *I will panic and you know it.*

"Not if I am with you."

Iya Greta emerged from the shade of the chimney, her hand extended for me to take. Where the valor to move came from, I did not know, only that my legs shuffled forth of their own accord. Taking her hand, soft and warm, I allowed Greta to lead me within the chimney. I crawled, shimmied, climbed, and slid as we turned in and out of different tiny passages.

Where are you taking me, I wondered, doing everything I could to distract myself from the panic gnawing at my edges.

"First, to a place where a friend awaits. From there, under things where the magic awaits. After that, forever away".

That sounds nice, I thought, finally beginning to succumb to the sway of my fever. The endless night abated as we exited the crawlspace and into a hollow not much bigger than a broom closet. Looking around I barely noticed the dozens of other tunnels that fed in and out of the hollow, nor did I wonder about the lamp and its welcoming light. Instead, as Greta bid me to sleep, I crawled past clothes and things and into a nest of blankets—sinking into a deep, deep slumber.

I was awoken from the doldrums of my respite by one angry and panicky girl. "Bastard!" she said shaking the last bits of sleep away from me. "How did *you* find my hideout?"

"Huh?" I grunted, bleary-eyed. Upon waking, I sensed two things. First, the pain in my mouth. Then, her presence. She was still shaking me. Frantic. Tense. Although I wanted to look about and figure out where I was, she captured all of my attention. Recognition passed between us. It was Rutoff—the brazen girl I had once met in the caves. The same one who had been there one moment and then gone the next.

"Good, you're up. You've got some answers to give and quickly," she said tersely.

Unable to speak, I made a noise that mostly registered the pain of my still-fresh wound.

Her eyes fell to my mouth. Ashamed, I closed my eyes and took a ragged breath. Perhaps sensing my agony, Rutoff softened just a little. Just a moment earlier she looked ready to beat me and now she just looked sorry.

"Never mind how you got here. Were in some deep sarding skat." It was then that I realized the hollow was not glazed with the filter of my dazed awakening but was rapidly filling with smoke. "Do you realize you led them to my hideout? They're trying to smoke us out."

Echoing in the distance, came the bark of baying hunting hounds. Rutoff looked white as a ghost. Gripping the scalpel, I turned and pointed at one of the tunnels.

"Why should I trust you?" she asked. "You led them here *and* I have no idea where that one goes yet. Do you realize how close I was to finding a way out? I nearly had it all mapped!"

Again, I pointed.

She threw her hands up and screamed.

It dawned on me that she couldn't see Greta there, motioning for us to follow.

I'll have to show her then!

I clambered up to the chute, waving for Rutoff to hurry, plunging into the darkness.

Rutoff yelled again, this time a fuming mess of frustration and despair. It was only a moment more before the light of her lamp illuminated the way and she was at my heels.

INTO THE DEEP

Halfwit

"Where are we going," Rutoff hissed, followed by the clang of her lamp against stone. I growled a deep and throaty response. Even that hurt. Couldn't she see that I had as much of an idea as she? Of course not. As far as she was concerned, I was leading this hasty crawl into the deep. I motioned for her to follow, which she did, and if not on the account of trust, then on the lack of smoke along our path.

Greta led us through a winding series of junctions, deeper, and deeper down.

"This is lessgood," Rutoff said. "We need to go *up* not *down*. Would you slow a bit? It's harder for me to squeeze through here."

I did not.

She cursed and followed, pulling herself free from the tunnel and into a strangely shaped cavern.

"Almighty," she breathed, her words trailing off in wonder.

All around us, in the walls, twinkled a golden blanket of constellations. Minerals and metals so precious and abundant I felt like a knight in dragons hoard. Luminescent insects crawled blindly across the ceiling on spindly legs, with antennas as long as my big finger. One of them dropped onto Rutoff's shoulder and she screeched. Gently, plucking the glowing creature into the palm of my hand, I set it on a small outcropping and watched as it wandered away. Patting Rutoff's shoulder, I pointed after Greta who stood above another chimney, waiting for us to follow.

"Don't touch me!" Rutoff snapped, pulling away. Sniffing, she looked about. "There had better be more to this. An *actual* way out."

Shaking my head, I ignored my throbbing fever and chased after Greta. Doing as my compeer, I pulled myself to a seat and slid down the chute, feet first. The butterflies raced in my belly as I quickly slid out of control, the chute becoming steeper, smoother, and slicker. I was falling. My back bucked the wall and I could just use my feet to control my descent. Shades of black and gray whooshed before me until I popped out of the chute, tumbling down an open slope, and crashing into a painful heap. Touching the lump in my pocket, I marveled that the scalpel had somehow not pierced my thigh.

"Lessgood! *Lessgoooooooood!*"

Rutoff crashed into my back, her lamp breaking and the light extinguishing. Clearing my pounding head, I shakily found my feet.

Light, true as day, poured into this great cavern from a massive sinkhole overhead. I laughed with joy until I realized it was impossible to climb out of this forsaken hole. We were in an unworldly place. The floors and the walls were made of one great piece of metal. Somehow formed with perfect slopes and no joining pieces. A cavern so large it could easily fit three or

WALKTALL

four of the largest ships that would dock in Hasbal's bay. But most strange of all was what awaited us at the center of this place.

"Where, in all of the deep, have you taken us?" Rutoff gasped, joining me at the lip of the perfectly square hole.

Below us, crafted in successive platforms was an absence of space, widest at the top and narrowest at the bottom. At its base floated what I could only describe as a flame, not flame. It had no source as a fire might and it seemed to float just above the ground. It was light blue and was visible in the same way that heat off of cobblestone on a sweltering summertide day was. Stairs, also made of that same piece of metal zigzagged from the top to the bottom.

Come. . . Greta sang.

"Are you insane?" Rutoff asked, grabbing me by my sleeve. "We lesscan go down there. Look at it!"

I did as she said and I heard Greta's voice again.

Grabbing Rutoff's hand, I tried to pry it loose but to no avail.

"I'm putting my foot down, idiot. We have to find a way out of here and you're going to help."

Just as the words left her lips another sound echoed across the cavern. The sounds of baying hounds trumpeting in triumph, followed by a sprinting approach, heralded by the sound of claw scraping upon metal.

"There! Get 'em!" exclaimed the Bad Man.

IZAIC YORKS

Whirling about, to our horror, we watched as the two hounds closed the distance, launching into the killing lunge.

Wailing incoherently, I pulled free of Rutoff, stepping between the beasts and her. If there was ever a time for my powers to work, now was it. The beasts drove me to the ground, but only one was able to sink its teeth into my arm; the other tumbled over the side, howling all the way to its crunching end.

Something whizzed past us. Musket fire. I didn't hear Rutoff scream. She had to be alright.

Grasping the hound by the nape of its collar, I screamed something primal, as it frenzied its head back and forth, making mincemeat of my arm. Somehow I managed to hold firm, eliciting a whine from the murderous mutt.

Go! I thought with all the force I could muster—praying that my magic would work. *You don't want us! You want to stop the Bad Man.* I impressed every memory and every hurt they had inflicted me with, transferring it upon the poor beast.

The hound unlocked its jaw and released me with a whine, its ears flat upon its head. Licking me once along my injury, it turned tail and charged after its master.

"Stop! Stop! What is this," the Bad Man yelped, imploring it with every command to turn back to its task. Still, the hound did not cease. Raising his musket, he fired. Still, the hound did not cease. Down both of them went as the mongrel's body became like a missile and its teeth found his throat. The

WALKTALL

Bad Man's scream was short-lived and the hound's final whimper long, as it succumbed to its wound.

"Are you all right?" Rutoff asked. I nodded. Shaking, white as a sheet, she helped me to my feet. "That looks doublebad," she said examining my arm. Tearing a strip of cloth from her shirt, Rutoff cinched it tightly about the wound, tutting all the way. "I wish I could have boiled that first."

I raised an eyebrow.

"I was apprenticed to a physician once. The old man caught me stealing supplies to treat the beggars and sent me on my way."

I stared and she shuffled her feet.

"Turns out the beggar lessused my gift and was selling them on the black market."

I nodded—sounded like the streets to me.

"What am I blithering on about," Rutoff scowled, suddenly remembering where we were. "We have to get out of here. He came from there," she said, pointing at an arched gate. "I doubt we should go there. And the way we came is too high up, but. . ."

"Come," *Greta sang.*

My eyes flicked to the slow dancing flame, not flame below. I pulled Rutoff's arm.

"Youlessserious?"

I nodded, setting my jaw.

"Oh, Almighty be merciful," Rutoff shivered. "Fine, you have gotten us this far."

Nodding, we ran down the stairs as fast as we could manage, towards the mystery below.

STRANGE AND MAGICAL

Halfwit

I was alive, fueled by mystery, grit, and grace. My body was in agony with every step and my head throbbed like the beating of the clocktower, assuring me that I was still alive.

"Come," Greta called.

I was not far. My hand, clenched and unclenched remembering the ghost of her touch.

"Hurry up," Peter insisted.

I did. I was so close to the flame, not flame I could see the eddies swirling within it. Mysterious bubbles and formations, unknown to adults, and yet perfectly at home in my child, not child's mind.

"Ja, ja, ja, the Mal'svoloc lives on within you," Harold breathed warmly.

My Prime. My eyes watered, swimming with the emotion that he had chosen me, and that by grace alone I had survived.

Breathless, I stood below the flame, not flame. I wondered what sort of wonderful magic was doing here. Then again all the great fairy tales had magic in the deepest and most unexpected places. Diffused sunlight washed over it all, emitting a prismatic array of angelic rainbows that painted all beneath the flame, not flame. I was so taken by the wash of my compeers radiating from the mysterious source, that I almost missed everything else about me.

"Almighty," Rutoff gasped, clapping a hand over her mouth. The floor was littered with bones, picked clean, bleached white. Around the base of the hole were six obelisks, repugnant and built of crude stone; attached to these ugly things, bound by chains driven into the stone, were two other children—one didn't breathe and the other babbled wildly at us.

"First student? No, Yegor?" I asked, disbelieving my eyes.

"Please, please, please," the Big begged, flecks of spit spraying from his lips. His arms, emaciated and weak, were strung by the chains above his head, and his body no longer bore the strength that it once had.

"Please, Second Student," Yegor cried. "It takes me, it takes me. I dun' want the Deep. I'm losing myself."

Rutoff touched my good arm. "We should run. Look at what this thing has done to him and to. . ." she nodded at the other Little, dead on his chain, like a cod upon the fisherman's line.

I shook my head emphatically. We had come this far, I was led this far, and I *had* to trust my compeers.

"Fine, whatever you are going to do, make it fast." The sounds of hounds and shouts echoed from somewhere not so far. Looking about I tried to find another chimney, another hiding place, some reason that they must have brought me here, but there was nothing.

WALKTALL 123

"Hurry," Rutoff whined.

"Please, please, please, I will do doubleplusanything, Second Student!"

At a loss of what else to do, I reached for the flame, not flame—the source of my compeer's voices.

Even though I was too short to reach, it did not matter, a column of shimmering light poured onto me, like water from a cup. I stumbled, compelled by the power of the flame, not flame. Enveloped in its grasp, sweet as *hverbraud* pulled from the ground, and laced with honeyed love. I rose higher and higher, lifted up and into the glowing heart of the magic. Like sinking into the cradle of a tub drawn with warm water, I entered into a place between here and there. A place all to its own.

All that I knew and all that I was disappeared unceremoniously. Notions of myself were wiped away as easily as gift tokens from the purses of unwitting marks. Like rotten skin shed with the rough of a pumice stone, or a prayer given on the breath of the Almighty, I became free. No longer was I the terrified child, bound behind the walls of my psyche, but a complete being. There no longer was an end to who I was but instead an unbroken circle between myself and creation. I would have lost myself in that eternal bliss, nurturing as a mother's embrace, were it not for Hair Harold.

He appeared to me in the fractal distillation that was my mind, but not as I knew him. Light, pure and eternal, diffused all that he was. Yet still I knew him by the brush of his soul.

"Halfwit," he said soft and loud all at the same time. "You who came and never willingly betrayed us. . ."

"Who never judged us," Peter said, flickering into view.

IZAIC YORKS

"And who befriended us all," Greta sang, appearing from nowhere and everywhere.

"I only did as any compeer should," I said. Slapping my hands over my mouth, I laughed hysterically and then cried. "My tongue! My tongue!" I exclaimed.

"Only while you are here can it be so," Peter said.

"Oh," I said, my face falling flat.

"That's not true," Greta said, "but it's not like he would pick the alternative."

"Ja, ja, ja, I think not."

"What do you mean?" I asked, taking Greta by the hands. "You mean I could be made whole again?"

"In the flesh? Yes."

"But being whole in the soul is far better," Peter added.

"I lessknow what you mean," I said, confused by it all.

"How could you?" Harold sighed. "Know this, we have the strength to save you and heal you. But if we do both, then I fear we won't be enough to save your friend as well. Does that make sense?"

I nodded. I felt the way in which Greta massaged my hands, renewed and without blemish. I held my breath. *I can be whole. It's so simple a thing.* And yet I knew I could never do it. I couldn't save just myself. It wasn't who I was. Squeezing my eyes, I shook my head and cursed my weakness.

WALKTALL

Halfwit indeed!

"Na, na, na. Never were you truly," Harold said, clapping me on the back. "And never were you Brun Torvold."

"You know my name?" I asked, slack-jawed.

"Ja and even better, I know who you truly are," Harold smiled.

Peter laughed, a twinkling thing, perfect and strange to hear from a boy's mouth—not that he was one any longer. "Here, there is no end between you and us." He was right I knew them as infinitely as they must know me. Harold the Protector, Peter the Helper, and Greta the Lover: Prudence, Hope, and Charity.

"And you, Torvold the Loyal," Greta sang, in a voice that could make th titans weep. "You must go, the Bad Men will soon arrive, we can sen them."

"But how?" I asked. "There is no way out of here."

Harold smiled rays of light. "Loyal, you who has so little faith. It was y who kept us from becoming one with the Almighty, who so indeli marked us, and it is you to whom we repay. Have faith."

"Faith? I lessknow what that is?"

"Ja. Return to Hasbal and one day you shall know."

Around me the eddies of magic began to fade, not like the quench of a c; dle, or the decay of a leaf, but instead like the fermentation of fruit—r and sweet.

"Wait!" I cried into the dwindling infinite. "What about Yegor, can you free him?"

"I don't think you need our help for that. Farewell Loyal, farewell."

And then all was gone. I felt the ground under my own two feet once more, and the brittle burn of air across my shorn tongue. Again I stood beneath the flame, not flame.

"Damn," Rutoff said, cursing over the much louder, much brasher melody of howls and shouts. "Sard me twice and stuff me in a barrel. You're back!" She said, smacking me in the face. Under her arm, supported by her, was Yegor. He could hardly stand without his knees knocking against one another or his fingers rubbing among themselves.

I cocked my head.

"Really? You go into that *thing* and you're going to act confused now that he is free? Boys are idiots! I *have* picked locks before," she said, motioning to the empty chains hanging from the obelisk. "Now please tell me that you found a way out, 'cause that's the only thing keeping me sane!" Hardly a breath after she finished her sentence the flame, not flame, erupted into light and a great fluttering shape emerged from within. Wings of silver, body as blue as the sea, and translucent as the flame, not flame, came a butterfly the size of a horse. It fluttered beside us. "Almighty above!" Rutoff exclaimed, wringing a hand through her hair. Both she and Yegor's gaze remained fixed on the magical creature, but I knew the gift for what it was, and scrambled up the body and onto its back.

I motioned for them to follow.

WALKTALL

"No, no, no, no no no!" she cried. "I have had enough of this, I would rather—" Musket fire cut her words short as a platoon of Bad Men arrived at the lip of the pit. Bits of lead sounded around us and the air above filled with the mists of war. Letting go of her, Yegor had no complaints about joining me. I motioned for her to hurry. Hounds howled, making haste down the stairs and straight for us. "Oh, damn you and damn me!" she exclaimed. Scurrying behind Yegor she wrapped her hands around his waist.

Jolting with each flap of the wing, the butterfly rose higher and higher, climbing past the snapping hounds and awed Bad Men. Looking up, towards the sinkhole and the sky above, my heart leaped for joy—until the butterfly faltered.

OURS IS OURS

Loyal

"No!" Rutoff wailed, covering her head as a spray of musket fire sliced the air about us. "We're so close!" she yelled, pointing at the sinkhole overhead. But instead of flying higher, we were struggling just to maintain altitude. The butterfly flapped in erratic circles, threatening to buck us.

"Un them, I say!" Liverspots cried, standing in the heart of the Bad Men. I could just see the white of his eyes, but the terror was plain to see. Slapping his men, he cajoled them to hurry with their reloading. Again, the butterfly tried to fly higher, and again it sank. I felt my insides curling down to my toes. I knew why we weren't ascending and what the solution was—so did Yegor.

"We're to heavy," he said, "one of us has to sacrifice."

"What?" Rutoff said, "That's madness! They'll be unned."

"It will be swift if they fall," Yegor explained.

"Who would it be? How would we even choose?"

I clenched my eyes and held my breath.

"You lessmean, no, no! I helped you, compeer," Rutoff said.

WALKTALL

"But you are lessfamily. Halfwit and I are *Mal'svoloc*. We are brothers who would never leave one another! Right, Halfwit?"

I craned to see them—Yegor had a crazed look on his face—struggling against one another, all while trying to keep a hold of the butterfly.

"I saved you," Rutoff moaned, as another volley scored the air. The butterfly dropped further, a fine pinprick now spotting it's silvered wing. Below us the hounds snarled and the badmen gnashed their teeth.

Why! Why! Why—

"You have to help me! Rutoff shrieked, "I could have turned you in but I lessdid!"

"Na! Help me. We're brothers, Halfwit! It's what Harold would have wanted!

Something within me snapped at the mention of Harolds name. *How dare you! You betrayed us all!* Memories of Peter, bleeding on the cavern floor, soured my mind. I imagined Greta crying in our cell. This and more bubbled over in a reign of rage.

Unfortunately for Yegor, that's not what he saw as I pulled the scalpel free.

The Big yipped for glee, the white of his teeth showing bright in the ray of sunlight, all the while, believing that I must have chosen his side. Turning his ruined eye to me, he gloated victorious over Rutoff. "Yes! Ours is ours and theirs is mostours! That's my Halfwi—"

The rest never did make it out of his mouth as I plunged the blade into him. Over and over and over. I painted the world in his blood, or so it felt, and the only reason I didn't continue was because he fell—bucked by the butterfly. Silver wings beat the air like sticks to a drum. We rose faster than the Bad Men could reload.

Up.

Up.

Up and out.

And yet all I could do was look. Was stare.

Down.

Down.

Down, at Yegor's broken body, and then we were gone—whisked away by the great butterfly.

Ours is ours, I thought over and over again. At times it was a bitter thought and at other times an empty one.

Tears touched my eyes as cotton clouds peeled away to show the sun in all its glory. "Where are we going?" Rutoff finally asked, after some time had passed and the sun had begun its final dip to the west.

I shrugged and pointed at my mouth.

"Oh. Yea. Sorry," she said sheepishly. "I guess you couldn't even tell me your name if I asked."

I smiled weakly and shook my head.

"Hmm. Well, thank you, I lessknow why you chose me back there, but thank you."

WALKTALL 131

I nodded.

"Can I tell you my name?"

I nodded.

"Sjen Freidis. I am so tired," she yawned, leaning into me. "Do you mind if I sleep?"

I shook my head.

"Alright, wake me if anything happens, or we arrive, or *whatever.*"

Before I could nod, she was already asleep and snoring softly into my ear.

On we flew and flew and flew. Crossing pink skies that turned to midnight blue, painted by the weaving greens of the Almighty's breath. If anyone were to look up, then they would have seen an ordinary butterfly traversing the starry sky. To the discerning eye, however, they would have seen something not quite right. A silver ghost, with flapping wings that didn't quite hide the pinpricks of heavenly light that it should've obscured. And to the superstitious, I imagine we looked like fairies, escaping from the clutches of the Tall-Men and their deep places.

Either was fine by me.

Small as I was, mute as I was, I now understood who I was.

Spying the curling waves of the sea, flecked with caps of white, and tracing the air with its salty mark, I smiled and sat just a little taller. Patting the butterflies back, I gave thanks to my compeers and shed the last of my tears.

I was free. I was home. I was Loyal.

IZAIC YORKS

And at last, I was happy.

EPILOGUE

Finishing the tale, I was neither relieved, nor happy, nor sad—I simply was.

Dirk Ava read and reread the last bits while I wiped the ink from my fingers and stretched away the spasms in my hand. I had never written anything so long before and I hoped I hadn't mucked it up too much. By now the room was at more than capacity, warmed by the heat of bodies pressed close together. Greth Jorgen, my dying friend's brother-in-law, read from behind Ava. He had not come until later in my recounting and was surely lost. The girl who had first brought us sat on the other side of the bed, the lantern resting on the plication of her mourning dress, looking nearly as pale as her dying mother. Then there was the physician, an aged man, steeped in the folk wisdom of his hamlet. "Her time is near," spoke the man, peering at her through frail-looking spectacles. No one paid him any attention.

Ava murmured the last lines of my story like an incantation whispered on a gloomy night. Setting the pen beside my cup of cold milk tea, my breath quivered within my chest. Taking Freidis by the hand I felt the wintertide chill that had taken root in her body. She already felt like a corpse, and beneath the pox of bursting red was a woman the color of aged ash.

"Oh, Mute," Ava whispered. "I suspected but I had no idea. . . I have so many questions, but it's not the time, is it?"

I shook my head, never taking my eyes off the woman I once called Rutoff.

Ava nodded.

"I still don't get it," frowned Greth Jorgen. "This explains so much about sissy but are you sure you remember that right? Magic and ghosts? Seems fanciful. A little too convenient."

Ava affixed him with a glare that had him stuttering out his words.

"What I mean to say is I once had a boyhood friend whose pup was mauled by a grizzly, and he himself barely escaped with his life. He wasn't right for nearly a month and the whole time he claimed a troupe of elves saved him from the beast. I'm sure that's what he remembers, even if it's not what happened."

Ava's glare only intensified, and the man stilled, holding his tongue for the moment.

In a way it was hard to believe and looking back it had been a sudden end to a horrid nightmare. Still, the time spent in that wicked place had been anything but quick. Maybe I had imagined the ending. Maybe it had been a sudden end to a long nightmare, but from the eyes of a child, it had been so exciting it had come with the blur and the intensity of celebrating one's naming day. In my experience, the most wondrous endings came suddenly and without explanation. Though our escape had been enigmatic at the time, now decades later it made some semblance of sense. Still, true magic would always be bound in a certain air of mystery and symbolism—no amount of inquiry would ever put that to rest. The more one pried into the magic, the more questions seemingly turned up.

WALKTALL

135

"It makes little sense," Greth Jorgen said, clearing his throat. "What was the point of it all?"

I shrugged, laughing a short and rugged sound. *What was the point indeed? Why the suffering?*

"Some people are just evil," said the girl in the gap of silence. We all looked at her. She blushed and lowered her head, saying, "That's what Mama says."

"Yes, and she was a wise woman," Greth Jorgen said.

"Her breathing is staggered and weak," spoke the physician at last—announcing the obvious once more. "Would you open the window? Let the Almighty gaze upon her soul."

Greth Jorgen moved mechanically to the shades and parted them. Light from the aurora borealis flooded the room, painting it strokes of diffused and shimmering greens.

"The oil is almost gone," moaned the girl, and as if in response the lantern light flickered and fluttered in a silent fuss. "Mama told me never to let it go out at night!" The girl jumped to her feet and was almost at the door when the physician made his proclamation: "Almighty rest her soul, lest it go to the Deep. She has departed."

"Come back, Ingrid," Greth Jorgen said, scooping the tearful child into his great arms. Carrying her back to her mother, Greth Jorgen's footsteps were heavy across the creaking wood, but not nearly as heavy as the girl's wails.

"Say your goodbyes," Greth Jorgen said. "Your mother deserves as much." Turning to address us the man added, "Lord Ascendant, compeer, your condolences are welcomed, but could we have a moment to ourselves?"

"Take all the time you need," Ava said, promising a hero's funeral for Freidis.

Once outside of the house and in the bluster of the rising wintertide storm, did I realize I had taken the lamp. The light had gone out, leaving only a blackened wick and sooty panes of glass. I knew this could not have been a device from back then, but it felt familiar in my hands. It was like holding a memory of everyone I had lost to the Bad Men and now Freidis too.

"We should light it. It would be good for Greth Ingrid," Ava said, returning to her action-oriented, no-nonsense, self. "Come on, Mute."

I shook my head.

"But it's not supposed to go out—"

I shook my head. I would not permit it. All things were meant to end.

"Alright, if you say so. I guess we will just wait then?"

I nodded, feeling the heat seeping from the lantern's metal.

Looking up into the night sky, I watched the dancing threads of the northern lights and marked the distant passage of a shadowy flight of butterflies. They weren't much bigger than the one we had ridden so many years ago, but they were solid creatures, born of flesh and blood. Standing as tall as my short body could manage, I imagined her flying away, asleep for the last time, finally ready to arrive at the halls of the Almighty.

GLOSSARY

Big

A street orphan, generally between the ages of ten and fifteen. Those who manage to live longer are either conscripted into the Lord Prime's army or recruited by other criminal syndications.

Little

A street orphan, generally between the ages of seven and ten. These children are generally used to pass information, trick, or pickpocket by the various street gangs. Additionally, children of this age are most suitable candidates for grooming into becoming Street Ladies or Painted Boys.

Street Lady

A woman whom men pay to go into a closed room with. Some Littles know what this means and certainly most Bigs do.

Painted Boys

Boys, usually Littles, who wear dresses, paint themselves in make-up and go behind closed doors to work like the Street Ladies.

Iridan

People with colorless, white eyes.

Hasbian

People with colored eyes

Hasbal

The once greatest city of the North. Citizens of the city-state are referred to as Hasbians

Teaser

Street gang language for anyone who distracts, obfuscates, or tricks the target of a score / con.

Strauss

An eastern word for street, assimilated into the Hasbian vernacular long ago.

Tall-Men

Fairy-tale creatures that resemble grotesquely tall men. It is said they capture fairies and children, not to eat, at least conventionally but to feed on the magic of their souls. It is said that is the source that gives them life and formidable stature.

Ascendant

Those who are blessed with a deep and ancient magic.

Ushanka

Tall furry hats, with long ear flaps that can either cozy around the face or be tied up high.

Strollers / Strolling Players

Performers and storytellers. Often with strange ideas and usually unwelcome by most good company.

Junto

The Lord Prime's highest-ranking cabal of Trusted. It is said that if the Lord Ascendant enforces the will of the Lord Prime, then it is the Junto who bends reality to meet it.

Sarding

An obscene word in reference to coital affairs.

Deep Ones

An affliction of evil, often manifesting as the voices heard in one's head. It is said to originate from evil spirits who escaped from the Deep. They look for refuge in the sinful and unclean due to the moral weakness of such souls.

Acknowledgements

Just like this novella, the list of those to recognize is small but impactful.

First, thank you beloved Courtney. You are the sweetest friend and love this side of heaven. Thank you for championing this work, helping me to feel like it matters, and is of The Good. Second, to my test readers, the final product is a testament to your wonderful feedback – thank you for stepping into this project with me. There would be no book without you. Third, to Angie, thank you for your thorough, editorial combing. I believe your work has taken *Walk Tall* to the next level. All mistakes are my own and not a reflection of your work. Fourth, thank you to my launch team. There would be no success without you.

Lastly, thank you to *you*, dear reader. A book is only half finished when it is published. Only the reader can finish it by consuming and experiencing the words in the theatre of their mind. Thank you for your support and time.

ABOUT IZAIC

Although he was born in Detroit, Michigan the Army brought the Yorks family to Tacoma, Washington in Izaic's younger years and he has considered the Pacific Northwest home ever since. His story in the sport of running has a different beginning than most of his colleagues as he didn't participate in athletics until high school, often choosing theater and musical interests over sports. It was not until he watched the 2008 Olympics with his physically disabled sister that he decided to pursue track —eventually leading to his current career as a professional athlete.

Izaic's passions however do not stop at the track but also extend into that of stories and writing. Izaic always knew he wanted to write novels but it was recently that he decided to dive in headfirst, after all every journey begins with a single step. He has spent years training and competing; and when he is not training he is dedicating countless hours to his passion of storytelling through writing fantastical stories, enjoying time with his family, and playing the occasional Dungeons and Dragons game.

Izaic likes to think of himself as a natural-born storyteller having loved sharing stories from a young age He thrives when he is able to express his creativity through writing or spoken narrative bringing his audience to new worlds. Izaic believes in writing stories that uplift and leave the readers filled with hope, and hanging on for the next page. He dedicates intentional time to perfecting the art of storytelling through regularly writing new stories, acting out new characters, and sharing his unique ideas with his wife who is sure to help him nix the bad ones.

Learn More at izaicyorks.com

You can find Izaic's full length high fantasy novel for purchase at his website. If you get the chance a rating and review goes a long way towards putting food on the table!

Afterword - Feeding the Indy Author

Hello! I hope this story brought you on a wild and unforgettable ride. As always it was with passion and desire to share a sliver of the Good, Great, Beautiful, and True that I wrote this story. But, I cannot write when I cannot eat. While purchasing a book goes a long way to sustainably bringing you new and fresh tales, it is a thriving ecosystem that ensures this boat stays afloat.

What do I mean?

Well, one of the biggest things that helps keep food on my table is ratings or reviews. In a sea of books, this is the one thing that assuredly turns heads. The more ratings and reviews (positive & negative) the more likely new readers are willing to try out my books. It takes less than five minutes to head to Amazon or Goodreads, using the book name in the search, and clicking the number of stars you believe this story is worth. With that in mind, I must humbly ask. . . Could you please leave a rating or review?

Sincerely & With Gratitude

Izaic Y

P.S. You can stay in the know regarding future books, audio projects, book club resources, and other fun things by visiting my website at izaicyorks.com and subscribing to my newsletter.

Also By

Set Two Decades After Walktal

Revolution cometh.

The sounds of Valor shall resound and pierce even the deepest reaches of the undercity, and not a soul will remain untarnished...

* * *

Hasbal, The City of Lights is no longer the capital of industry, but instead, a place frozen in time as its denizens reach ever towards the promised utopia.

Ghost-Who-Walks is on the run from his past and he is dreadfully tired. Centuries have come and gone, and yet he still can not escape his duty. When called upon once more The Ghost will have to decide if he has the courage to fight one last time.

Dirk Ava wants what any other teenage girl might. Someone to love her. The freedom to do as she wishes, and the chance to overthrow the Lord Prime. The daughter of an extremist freedom fighter in a group known as the Shields of Valor, Dirk Ava has been groomed for war from an early age. But when a deep magic awakens within Ava, her entire life is turned inside out. Ava's coming-of-age story sets her on a soul-shattering quest to master her powers, overcome betrayal, and kill the Lord Prime.

CYBERPUNK X BLACK MIRROR X BLADE RUNNER

Join Hal, one of the top track stars in the solar system. He has only ever known life as a ghoul, with a life debt that he can never repay...

That is until the Cartel buys his freedom in return for a simple task that only his lab-grown, enhanced body might just survive.

An Audio Book / Drama

Learn About All Upcoming Projects at izaicyorks.com

OR

Printed in the USA
CPSIA information can be obtained
at www.ICGtesting.com
LVHW030154141023
761050LV00016B/286